MW00720335

MISSION
BETRAYED

DAVID FRANKLYN

ccp

First Edition April, 2012

Published by Caribbean Chapters Publishing
P.O. Box 4133, Saint Peter, Barbados
www.caribbeanchapters.com

Edited by Carol A. Pitt

ISBN: 978-976-95295-7-1 paperback

ACKNOWLEDGEMENTS

The author is indebted to his cousin, unnamed, who told him of the disarming of the militia that day in October 1983 when afterwards the militia was informed that Maurice Bishop was under house arrest. His narrative of how he experienced this event as a betrayal, his description of his participation in the Heroes of the Homeland Maneuvre in 1981 and befriending a girl from Grand Roi helped to inspire this narrative. The author is indebted to the other persons whose narratives informed this story.

The author also wishes to express gratitude to Carol Pitt who edited the manuscript, suggested improvements and made the work coherent and publishable

PREFACE

The Grenada Revolution (March 13th, 1979 to October 19th, 1983) and its tragic implosion are defining events in the Caribbean experience. These events have been largely misunderstood. As a student at the University of the West Indies, both in Barbados and Jamaica, the author discovered that fellow students from other Caribbean islands were fascinated with the Grenada revolution and hungry for knowledge of what it was like to have lived during those times and to have witnessed these events.

This novel attempts to answer these questions through the story of the main protagonist, who is a composite of actual characters known to the author, particularly a cousin—who will not be named because the author does not have his permission—and through the author's own personal experience of the events.

The narrative is essentially about a generation of Grenadians who believed that they had discovered their mission, as Frantz Fanon said every generation should, and sincerely devoted itself to fulfilling that mission, only to end up betraying it, a possibility Fanon also recognized.

It is hoped that readers will learn a valuable lesson from this narrative, particularly the need to avoid putting ideology and party before people and allowing emotion to triumph over reason and common sense in times of crisis.

There are two characters in the novel that may appear fictional: 'Miss Praise-the-Lord', and a seer who appears in the courtyard of the Sauteurs police station on the morning of the revolution predicting its demise. They are real characters witnessed by the author in their roles.

The reader may also wonder why the Carifta Cottages, where part of the novel is set, was attacked during the U.S. military action in October 1983. The circumstances surrounding the attack were explained to the author by an ex-paratrooper, R. D. Walker, who participated in the U.S military action in Grenada. We are thankful to him for his assistance, and his explanation is put in the mouth of one of the characters towards the novel's end.

The author hopes that through experiencing this novel readers will gain an understanding of what it was like to have lived through the Grenada Revolution—through those radical times—and witnessed history unfolding in real time.

In writing this narrative the author reflected on
the words of a song/poem by Tracy Chapman,
Telling Stories:
'*There is fiction in the space between the lines on
the page, the memory...*'

This narrative is based on actual historical events
and draws upon the author's own experience and
rememberance of things he witnessed in Grenada
between March 1979 and October 1983.

The characters are based on actual persons known
to the author and are composites of real people,
but the work as a whole is largely the product of the
creative imagination and is not intended as a history.

Some dialogue and events have been compressed
to convey the substance of what was said or what
occurred, and, in some cases, have been recreated
from memory.

This novel is dedicated to my children
Denzil, Adel and Amon, and the
children of their generation.

* PART ONE *

CHAPTER 1

October 19th, 1983, 7:28 p.m.

WHEN he got home on the evening of October 19th, 1983, Comrade's cottage was dark.

He was staying at the Carifta Cottages, a housing complex that was built by the former Prime Minister Eric Gairy in 1968 to house participants of the CARIFTA games which were held in Grenada that year. A fellow comrade who lived in one of the cottages had loaned it to him, as he was traveling to Moscow on a mission. Other comrades lived in the other cottages.

Everyone called him Comrade because he loved referring to others as 'comrade' all the time, and because everybody saw him as a true revolutionary, a true comrade. He was tall, strongly built, energetic, and very dark like his father John-John, a notorious policeman of the old days.

The cottage felt lonely, but he did not switch on the lights. He fumbled to his bedroom, feeling exhausted and empty. He threw himself on the bed and switched on his transistor radio. The night was growing old.

It had been the most dramatic day of his life and the drama had either been a farce or a tragedy; he could not yet decide, for it was still in play and he wondered how it was going to end.

The day had started with mass demonstrations, mostly of school children and other young people.

A crisis had broken out some days earlier when people learned that Maurice Bishop, the charismatic leader of the revolution that had occurred in 1979, had been placed under house arrest by members of his own party because of a dispute over leadership. They suspected a conspiracy by perceived hardliners to remove Bishop from power.

Comrade wondered whether the mass demonstration he had witnessed this morning was a demonstration of the people's love and support of the 'revo', as it was popularly referred to, or a demonstration of their love and support of Maurice Bishop, or both. He knew that Bishop's charisma largely gave the revo its legitimacy at home and in the wider Caribbean region, if not the world, and that to many local people Bishop embodied the revo—they were one and the same.

The chanting marchers had gone to free him from his house arrest, but Comrade had not joined them, fearing that the other side who had put him under house arrest would authorize the soldiers of the People's Revolutionary Army—the PRA—to open fire on the demonstrators, though over the years Bishop had assured the people that the guns of the revo would never be turned on them.

At around 9:30 the radio broadcast was interrupted and the voice of General Hudson Austin came on air to make an announcement. Comrade listened attentively with chills running down his spine as General Austin recapped the events of the day.

<<*This morning at 9:00 am, a crowd led by Unison Whiteman, Vincent Noel and two businessmen stormed Maurice Bishop's home. The soldiers guarding the Mount Royal road had instructions not to fire on the people. The people therefore broke through the barrier and stormed through the gate of the house. Again the soldiers were instructed not to fire on the people, but to fire above the people's heads.*>>

Comrade nodded. This was exactly what he had heard from people who had participated in the storming of Mount Wheldale, Maurice Bishop's house. General Austin continued:

<<The crowd, realizing that the soldiers had instructions not to fire on them, broke into the house. Maurice Bishop went with them and then led the crowd of innocent people to seize Fort Rupert, the headquarters of the armed forces...>>

Earlier in the day Comrade had been disappointed when he looked up the street and saw the crowd heading towards the fort. Had there been a sudden change of plans? They were supposed to bring Bishop to the market square to address his supporters who were waiting there. Microphones had already been set up in anticipation of the address. The people were depending on Bishop to tell them his version of the reason for the crisis, reassure them that the beloved revo was not in danger, and tell them the way forward.

The market square had been the natural choice for such a gathering. It was a central location in downtown St. George's. It was used as a vendors' market for mostly agricultural products, and served the dual purpose of a bus terminal where you could get a bus to any part of the country. Preachers used it to preach sermons and politicians used it to hold political rallies. Carnival masqueraders gathered in the market square. In the old colonial days the colonial authorities used it to publicly hang people. Comrade had heard that it was even used as a place where slaves were auctioned in the old slavery days.

As he wandered around the market square that morning wondering why the crowd had gone up to the fort instead of taking Bishop to the square, he caught a glimpse of the towering grey monstrosity and saw people crawling all over it like crazy ants. It was on a promontory overlooking St. George's harbour and was named after King George, whom Comrade had heard was a crazy old king. The revolution had renamed it Fort Rupert after Maurice Bishop's father who had been shot to death during the pre-independence anti–Gairy struggle of 1973-1974, and made it the military headquarters of the People's Revolutionary Armed Forces.

Why had the crowd been led there? Had they

decided on a military solution to the crisis? Who were they who had taken this decision?

Even as Comrade was wondering this, General Austin said:

<<*They have disarmed the officers of the General Staff as well as the rank and file soldiers guarding Fort Rupert and have begun arming the crowd.*>>

"They did that?" Comrade cried in disbelief as General Austin continued:

<<*They declared their intention to arrest and wipe out the entire Central Committee and the senior members of the party and the entire leadership of the Armed Forces, as well as to smash the Revolutionary Armed Forces.*>>

As Comrade was digesting this information and concluding that the other side must have felt threatened, desperate, and must have panicked, the timbre of General Austin's voice changed and he said:

<<*At that point the Revolutionary Armed Forces were forced to storm the fort and in the process the following persons were killed: Maurice Bishop, Unison Whiteman, Vincent Noel,*

Jacqueline Creft, Norris Bain and Fitzroy Bain, among others.>>

Comrade sneered at this announcement. General Austin made it sound as if they had been killed in a crossfire or in action. Comrade had left Town that afternoon with the impression that Maurice Bishop and others had been executed. After the initial fire fight, there had been a lull. Survivors had poured down the hill bleeding and screaming:

"They open fire on us! They kill a lot of people!"

One man who was looking for a bus to take him back to Grenville had told him:

"People jump off the fort to escape the bullets! There were bodies everywhere! I saw a soldier herding Bishop, Jackie, Uni, Norris Bain and others to the upper level. He was shouting in glee: Is execution time!"

"Execution?" Comrade cried. Then he heard the sudden, short burst of gunfire and the man wailed:

"Oh God, they execute them! They execute Broder Bish and them!"

As Comrade lay in his bed and listened to

General Austin confirm the deaths of some of the most popular leaders of the revolution by what he believed to have been an execution, something in him died—a ray of hope, an old faith, a fervent spirit. He sat up suddenly with indescribable dread as General Austin made a harsh and chilling announcement. He announced the imposition of a twenty-four hour, shoot-on-sight, shoot-to-kill curfew, a word he pronounced as 'curfoo'.

<<*No one is to leave their house. Anyone violating this curfoo will be shot on sight.*>>

Comrade was stunned. Had he seen this coming? He hadn't. He had believed in the revolution and its leaders. He had faith in them, believed that they meant well and were united and intelligent, patriotic and rational. They would never do anything to harm the masses. Yet this was happening, and it was a very inhumane development. What was this? Surely it was not the revolution the people had supported— the revolution Bishop had embodied. This was something else, something undefined, something sinister.

Comrade recalled an encounter he'd had the

year before in the market square. He had gone there to buy a roti from an old Indian woman who made the best curry in Town.

A crowd was gathered around a preacher. Comrade pushed his way into the crowd to get a glimpse of this preacher. She was a black, middle-aged woman with a shrill voice, and she frequently interrupted her rant with shouts of "Praise the Lord!" She was slim, of medium height, with an attractive face. She was dressed in African print and her head was wrapped Spiritual Baptist style. She wore sandals.

What she was saying stunned and titillated her audience, and it troubled Comrade. She was not preaching a religious sermon. She was revealing insider information about what she alleged was happening within the leadership of the revolution.

"They are divided into factions," she alleged. "One faction is very aggressive. Lobbying, canvassing, getting its people in strategic positions in the government, the party, the army—Praise the Lord—Getting rid of Bishop supporters, criticizing Bishop for his lack of administrative leadership and organizational skills and his weakness in ideology—Praise the Lord—In the end Bishop will lose and the country will be put under heavy manners by the soldier boys and the hardliners."

Who is this woman? Comrade wondered. *How dare she say these things in public?* The revolution was very hard on people who spread propaganda calculated to undermine confidence in the leadership and destabilize the country. People had been detained just for being suspected of being destabilizers and spreading gossip. Yet this woman, who people referred to as Miss Praise-the-Lord, was openly making serious allegations of factional in-fighting, rivalries, conspiracies and power struggles among the leadership, and no one was arresting her. Who was protecting her? Who was feeding her this information? Was she mad or playing mad? Was her madness or perceived madness protecting her? If she was mad or perceived to be mad, no one would take her seriously. Was this what was protecting her? But people were taking her seriously. He overheard one woman telling another:

"Don't doubt her. She know what she saying. Bishop in trouble. The revo in trouble!"

But was the revolution really in trouble? In his

radio broadcasts to the nation, Bishop himself insisted that all was well, that the leadership was united as never before and that the only threat to the revo was imperialism.

As he lay in bed tormented by his reflections, Comrade realized that Miss Praise-the-Lord indeed knew what she was saying and was probably only playing mad to protect herself. But who was her source and protector? Who was she? Was she a seer? Seers were mostly Spiritual Baptists. They had visions and old people like his grandmother believed in them and said they could see far. They went about the country ringing a bell, sprinkling holy water and proclaiming "Sudden death! Sudden death! Hard times ahead with mother eating father and father eating mother! Storm winds coming! Batten down! Watch and pray! Watch and pray!"

His grandmother had warned him not to make fun of them, not to mock them, for they had powers—mystical powers. Comrade feared them. A comrade from St. Patrick's had told him that on the morning of the revolution an old woman, a notorious seer, had moved through the crowd that was gathered in the courtyard of the Sauteurs police station, proclaiming:

"Those who overthrow Uncle Gairy and calling it revolution go soon eat one another! They go turn their guns on one another. My mouth is goat mouth! What I say go come to pass. They go kill one another!"

The comrade had said: "I know what Grenadians go say. I make this up. I lying. But other people who were there and witnessed this thing could testify that I telling the truth."

Comrade reflected on this now and concluded that if the comrade was indeed telling the truth, this seer must really have the ability to see far. *Had she put a curse on the revo or had she had a vision of the future?* Whatever it was, he decided, seers were to be feared, and mad people or people playing mad were to be taken more seriously.

Comrade discovered the tears flowing from his burning eyes. He felt the warmth on his cheeks. He wept uncontrollably. He wondered why he was weeping and rationalized it by telling himself that he was weeping for Maurice Bishop and the others, including the innocent adults and schoolchildren who had died on the fort earlier in the day, and for the terrified nation that had been so cruelly put under a twenty-four hour, shoot-on-sight, shoot-to-kill curfew.

Then he decided that he was weeping for the revolution that had been so carelessly and treacherously betrayed.

He nursed this rationale for his weeping for a while, and then decided to face the truth and admit the real reason for it: he was weeping for himself, for his own tragedy and betrayal, for arresting his own father and detaining him on the order of his mentor, who Comrade now realized had betrayed him and betrayed his own dream of a free and just society, where everyone would have equal opportunity to prosper.

Dialectics had ordered him to arrest his father and he had done it for the sake of the revolution, and the revolution had come to this.

CHAPTER 2

October 25th, 1983, 3:15 a.m.

COMRADE was awakened by an explosion of thunder. He sat up in his bed abruptly. It was the 25th of October, his twenty-third birthday. It was the official end of the hurricane season and an unusual time for thunder, but sometimes the season extended to November.

He recalled past hurricane seasons in Grenada when he was growing up, when he would imagine the thunder splitting the world asunder. He would run to his grandmother to hide in the folds of her skirt, or if he had already gone to bed, cower under the sheet, hugging his pillow tightly. Thunder and lightning always frightened him then, and during the hurricane season they occurred together, threatening to split the world apart, bringing big trees crashing down.

His grandmother would come over to his bed and hug him to her, caressing his head as the thunder exploded and the lightning flashed.

Sometimes the wind would join in, blowing hard and howling. Then the rain would join in the mischief and beat on the roof like horses' hooves, and his grandmother would tell him stories.

One story she told him alleged that a hurricane was the anger and rage of two gods—Huracan, a god of the indigenous people who was angry that they had been betrayed, dispossessed of their islands and exterminated; the other was Shango, a god of thunder, angry that his people had been transported from Africa against their will in the holds of ships across the Atlantic, enslaved on plantations, and made to suffer every injustice man has ever imagined and committed against his fellow man. He was terrified of these angry gods.

"Child," his grandmother told him, "nature could be violent and destructive, but human beings could be even more violent and destructive. The year you were born, two presidents of the two superpowers were on the brink of destroying the world, but Papa God wasn't ready yet for the world to end, so He held their hands."

"On the brink of destroying the world?" He

queried. "How?"

"With nuclear weapons," she responded. "Weapons more explosive than thunder, with brighter flashes than lightning, with a more powerful force than hurricane wind and with the power to destroy every living thing for miles around and contaminate the water and the very air we breathe."

She still experienced the terror she had felt at that time as she and her son John John, Comrade's father, sat in their living room and listened to the countdown on the radio. Comrade was a baby then, without a care in the world, happily and innocently sucking on a morsel of sugar cane she had given him to keep him quiet.

Only days before, John John had brought this boychild to her and asked her to take care of him because the child's mother didn't want him and had dumped the baby on him. *Was he the child's real father?* Yes, he was. *Was he certain?* He was. The woman had been his girlfriend and he had done what he had done and got her pregnant.

October, 1962

The radio was saying that the Russians had placed nuclear missiles aimed at America on military bases in Cuba, that Cuba was only ninety miles from America, and that this was a provocation and an act of war, especially as Cuba was within America's sphere of influence.

Sphere of influence? Comrade's grandmother did not comprehend the meaning of the term.

John John had explained to her that there was a cold war on. *A cold war? Can a war be cold? Isn't war associated with heat?*

He told her that this war was called cold because the two superpowers were not directly physically engaged and the world appeared to be at peace. Their armies and navies and air forces were not battling each other in any direct and obvious way. Theirs was an ideological battle— an ideological rivalry; a contest over whose political and economic ideology and whose political system and way of life should dominate in the world.

John John tried to explain communism, capitalism and democracy to her. He tried to get her to understand the rivalry by alluding to local history.

He told her that in the days of Fedon in the late 1700s the rivalry had been between Britain and France, the two most powerful colonial rivals in the Caribbean. France, after their revolution, favoured a republican form of government, and Britain favoured the more traditional monarchial form of government. The French revolution promoted the idea of the Rights of Man and was willing to extend these rights to the enslaved populations of their colonies.

Britain referred to the French revolution's ideal of liberty and equality derisively as 'the leveling ideology of the French' and was determined to maintain its social hierarchy of superior and inferior classes and races and to defend and perpetuate the system of slavery in the islands. That was one of the reasons they fought to seize the French colony of St. Dominique and restore slavery there against the will of the uprising slaves who, like Fedon and others in Grenada and other British colonies, were inspired by the French revolution's ideal of liberty and equality to attempt armed revolution and free themselves.

"In the same way there are people who are

attracted to the ideals of communism and associate it with liberty and equality..." he told her, but John John himself knew better and supported capitalism and democracy as opposed to communism, and America as opposed to Russia.

The radio said that the American president's finger was on the button.

What button?

John John told her that if the president pressed it, it would trigger a nuclear war. And he would press it any time now, for Russian navy ships were steaming towards Cuba and the American military had been mobilized.

It was a tense moment and Comrade's grandmother prayed a desperate prayer, besieging Papa God to stop these arrogant madmen, for he had promised a world without end and if it had to end it would be his decision, his initiative, not the decision and initiative of mere humans—mere flesh and blood playing god.

She felt that her prayers were answered when the radio said that the two presidents were talking and exchanging cables, and when it announced that the Russian navy had turned around and was moving back towards Russia and that the Russian president had promised to remove the missiles from Cuba if the Americans promised not to invade Cuba.

She breathed a sigh of relief. The world would not end after all, not yet anyway. Not until Papa God decided that it was time. But what was the meaning of this sphere of influence? John John told her that the two superpowers had divided the world into spheres in which their particular ideology and way of life prevailed and which they both must respect and not interfere in. Cuba was physically within the American sphere of influence, so it was natural that the Americans were alarmed by their communist system of government and their alliance with Russia. Russia had provoked America by placing nuclear missiles in Cuba to give them the advantage of first strike in case of a nuclear war.

Comrade's grandmother understood a little, but her main concern was for her little grandson, only months old, whose only care in the world was sucking on this little piece of sugar cane he held in the tight little fist of his chubby right hand, experiencing in his innocence only the sweetness of life, oblivious to the bitterness.

Was this the world that he was going to grow up in? A world of rivalry between superpowers called a cold war? A world of nuclear weapons that could bring about an end to the world but for the mercy of Papa God? The poor little thing would be so vulnerable all his life and may be forced to choose sides, poor child. How could she protect him?

Her husband had not returned from the Second World War and her own father had died in the battle of the Somme in the First World War, which her grandfather had discouraged him from joining, as it was a war of European Kings and Tsars and Kaisers and Dukes and Earls and other nobles and European tribes, and was best left to them.

Would the poor child grow up fighting foreign wars as her father and husband had done? She knew of neighbours' sons who had joined the American military and fought in Korea "to divide that poor country into a communist north and a capitalist south" and in Vietnam where the communists were winning decisive battles.

John John had told her that all these wars were proxy wars of the cold war. She did not understand. He was her only child and had joined the police force as soon as he turned eighteen. He was tall enough, literate enough and tough enough, and he had a streak of cruelty in him that she felt certain he got from his father's side of the family, since no one on her family's side were brutes.

After his grandmother told him this terrifying tale of the time the world was on the brink of being destroyed by nuclear war, Comrade appreciated why he liked sugar cane so much and began to expand his understanding of the world.

At secondary school his older schoolmates debated the pros and cons of communism and capitalism and talked about the cold war. He learned about the non-aligned movement and explained it to his grandmother.

"It is a group of countries that have decided not to take sides in this Cold War, not to align themselves with either of the superpowers, but instead to follow a middle way."

"That make sense," she said. "We shouldn't take sides."

When, following the March 13th Revolution,

Comrade's friend Dialectics told him that the leadership had adopted communism to guide their line of march, were dedicated to building socialism and had aligned themselves with Cuba and Russia, he had been alarmed. Like Cuba, Grenada was within the American sphere of influence, so wouldn't this make the revolution vulnerable?

This concern was resolved for him when he heard a bold speech made by Maurice Bishop, the leader of the revolution, on Radio Free Grenada. It was April, 1979, a month after the revolution. Bishop was addressing the nation and was angry because of what he said were veiled threats against the revolution by the U. S. ambassador. He was indignant that the ambassador would warn Grenada against any friendship with Cuba.

Comrade had recorded and replayed the speech so often that he memorized it in its entirety. Its defiance was infectious, and while listening to it or reciting it, he had felt that same defiance. He would often quote his favourite parts to other comrades, pushing out his chest like a cockerel as he did so.

<<*Sisters and brothers, what we led was an*

independent process. Our revolution was definitely a popular revolution, not a coup d'etat, and was and is in no way a minority movement. We intend to continue along an independent and non-aligned path... We are a small country, we are a poor country, with a population of largely African descent, we are part of the exploited Third World, and we definitely have a stake in seeking the creation of a new international economic order which would assist in ensuring economic justice for the oppressed and exploited peoples of the world, and in ensuring that the resources of the sea are used for the benefit of all people of the world and not for a tiny minority of profiteers...>>

Then he would recite his very favourite part of the speech in his most defiant delivery:

<<Grenada is a sovereign and independent country, although a tiny speck on the world map, and we expect all countries to strictly respect our independence just as we will respect theirs. No country has the right to tell us what to do or how to run our country or who to be friendly with. We certainly will not attempt to tell any country what to do. We are not in anybody's backyard, and we are definitely not for sale... Though small and poor, we are proud and determined. We would sooner give

up our lives before we compromise, sell out, or betray our sovereignty, our independence, our integrity, our manhood, and the right of our people to national self-determination and social progress. Long live the revolution!>>

The other comrades would marvel at the way he managed to memorize this and many of Maurice Bishop's other speeches that were broadcast on Radio Free Grenada, delivered at rallies or printed in the Free West Indian or some other publication.

He explained himself.

"We don't have the speeches of Fedon. We were not present during that process in those long ago days, and no one has recorded them for us and for posterity, but we are this present generation. We living this history. This history unfolding in our time. So I recording these speeches and filing away the printed ones, and even memorizing some and keeping a journal of daily events. I capturing the moment in words, describing the atmosphere, recording thoughts and snatches of dialogue to help me remember and relive, so I can enlighten my children and grandchildren and people around the world."

CHAPTER 3

COMRADE was jolted back to the present as he heard the radio announcer calling on "one and all" to come out and fight the invaders, and to block all roads to impede the progress of the enemy. He agreed that this was what everyone should be doing—what they would have done had Maurice Bishop been alive and in power, but he grew tired of the announcer and switched the radio off.

He sat immobile in bed listening to the constant thunder and the explosions, expecting to see lightning, to hear the roar of wind and rain. He was puzzled that only the thunder was audible.

The thunder seemed concentrated to the south of the cottages, towards Point Salines, where local and Cuban construction workers were working on the site of an international airport that the People's Revolutionary Government was building, and in the Calliste and

Frequente areas. He had a crazy cousin working with the Cubans on the airport construction site and when he said that his life was 'as hard as Cuban daywork' you knew how hard his life was. He thought of this cousin and the hardworking Cubans now as the thunder exploded towards the south.

The thunder was constant. He checked the time. It was almost 6:00 in the morning. He went across the room, opened the window, and looked outside. The sun had risen. It was dawn and it was dewy outside. The view was always panoramic from the Carifta Cottages. You could see Grand Anse beach, the hotels behind the row of coconut trees, the sea, and a glimpse of St. George's.

Two planes thundered across the pale blue sky. Comrade blinked. They were not commercial planes. They looked and maneuvered like military planes—fighter jets.

Military planes! Wha' going on? He wondered.

He ran to the transistor radio on the bedside table and switched it back on. It was permanently tuned to Radio Free Grenada, the only station he had listened to since the revolution. It played lots of his favourite reggae music and calypsos from all over the Caribbean, including his favourite artist, Brother Valentino, a Trinidad-based calypsonian with Grenadian roots. It played revolutionary slogans and jingles like *'let dem come, let dem come, we will bury dem in the sea!'* 'Dem' referred to the Americans, otherwise known as the imperialists, natural enemies of socialist revolutions.

Radio Free Grenada used to announce the schedule of militia meetings all over the island until days ago when the militia was disarmed because of the crisis. It also broadcast the speeches of Maurice Bishop.

Six days earlier it had announced Bishop's death, along with the deaths of other prominent leaders of the revolution. Comrade shivered as he remembered this tragedy. He was among the crowd gathered in the market square waiting for those who had gone to free Bishop from house arrest and to bring him there to make a speech. Instead, the crowd and Bishop had gone to the fort.

Comrade remembered how terrified he was when gunfire broke out on the fort and he heard people screaming and saw some of them running down the road. The firing had stopped after a few minutes and there was silence. Then the silence was interrupted by a burst of sustained gunfire that lasted for around fifteen minutes.

He remembered how he had gasped in horror and wondered: *What is the meaning of this second burst of gunfire? Who are they shooting now?* The people in the market square began to disperse, shrugging their shoulders and saying with resignation that it was all over now, that Maurice Bishop was dead. They were sure of it. For what else could explain this second burst of fire but an execution by firing squad?

Then, as Comrade left the market square, he remembered with alarm the Amber and the Amberdines scenario and gasped. *It has happened as scripted. The government of Amber has split into factions and one faction has eliminated the other. Now there is only the invasion to follow to rescue American hostages. But who are these hostages? Where are they? Who is holding them hostage?*

He thought now of the American medical students at the school of medicine down at True Blue. No one was holding *them* hostage. Why would anyone hold them hostage? The members of the Central Committee would be stupid to hold them hostage, as this would only invite the wrath of their government.

He also recalled what he had said to a man walking beside him. "Comrade, do you remember Amber and the Amberdines?"

"Don't call me comrade!" the man replied, indignantly. "I am not a comrade. They release me from detention three weeks ago. I was considered a danger to the revolution and arrested and put under heavy manners. No, I have not heard of Amber and the Amberdines. Is that some kind of fruit like a granadilla or a manderine or tangerine?"

Comrade told him that it was the title of a U.S. military maneuver held in Puerto Rico some years ago that many thought simulated an invasion of Grenada.

The man nodded and said, "Well in that case I hope they come quickly and rescue us from ourselves. I once read somewhere some Trinidad writer saying that we black people are dangerous only to ourselves. You doubt him?"

Comrade had ignored the question and tried to change the topic.

"While you were in detention did you get to meet a man named John-John? A tall, dark, strapped man?"

"An ex-policeman?" the former detainee asked.

"Yes," Comrade confirmed.

"Ah, John-John. I remember him. He is a good man. A courageous man. He prayed all the time and comforted others, telling us we'll soon be freed. He was so optimistic. He admitted to some wrong-doings when he was an Inspector of Police during Gairy days, like beating up the leaders of the New JEWEL Movement, including breaking Maurice Bishop jaw with a baton and forcing the fella all you now call Dialectics head into a toilet bowl and flushing it. Firing teargas at demonstrators and bursting the heads of protesting schoolchildren with his baton and beating them with his bull pizzle. He say this was the real reason he was arrested and put in detention, and not for being a CIA agent. He swore he wasn't no CIA agent or counter-revolutionary and made us laugh when he say that the first time he heard of the CIA was in that Bob Marley song, Rat Race, in the line: Rasta nuh work for no CIA. He regretted all the wrong things he did as a policeman during Gairy days and forgave those who had him in detention, including his own son who he said was among the militia who came to arrest him and accuse him. You know this man?"

Comrade said: "I'm his son!"

"You are the son who arrested him, your own father?" Disbelief distorted the expression on the man's face.

"I am."

The man then quickened his pace and was soon far ahead of Comrade, putting as much distance between them as he could.

It had begun to grow dark and a jeep of People's Revolutionary Army soldiers stopped to give Comrade a lift. When they reached the man, they stopped to offer him a lift, but the man refused and bolted for the beach.

CHAPTER 4

COMRADE'S friend Dialectics had told him that the crisis started over a proposal by the Central Committee for joint leadership between Maurice Bishop and Bernard Coard, his deputy. The two would marry their strengths in the interest of the revolution. Maurice Bishop had at first agreed to the proposal, then reneged on it. This infuriated the members of the Central Committee.

That was the version the members of the Central Committee had tried to explain to the masses all over the country to justify their decision to put Maurice Bishop under house arrest.

"All-you must be crazy, comrade!" He told Dialectics. "Why all-you put the people hero under house arrest? This would inflame the people! They would rise up!"

"We expect them to rise up," Dialectics replied, "and we are prepared to deal with them."

"This will endanger the revo," Comrade argued, "it will open the door for imperialism to come in."

"The revolution already in trouble, Comrade. The economy not doing well, attendance at rallies is declining, productivity is down, membership of the National Youth Organization and the National Women's organization is down, the morale of the people is down, the revolution losing support. The Central Committee decided that this is due to the weaknesses in Maurice Bishop's leadership. He has charisma and he is a great orator, but he lacks strategy and organizational skills. The Central Committee proposed joint leadership of the revolution between he and Bernard as a solution to these problems. In this way they would marry their strengths. At first, he accepted the proposal, but afterwards he began to listen to his own fears and suspicions and the fears and suspicions of others that this was a ploy by the Central Committee to overthrow him and to seize power from him. Especially by Bernard who stands to benefit most. And so he reneged on his acceptance of the proposal and began to circulate a rumour that Bernard and his wife Phyllis are conspiring to overthrow him and seize power for themselves. So we decided to place him under house arrest for his own sake."

"Well, didn't you think before you acted that this would put the revolution in danger? Why this proposal of joint-leadership so essential to the survival of the revolution that you have to risk betraying the revolution to implement it? It doesn't make sense to me."

"We will explain our actions to the people," Dialectics replied.

"And will the people simply accept your explanation and agree with you that brother Bish deserves his house arrest? The people will believe the rumour. They never fully trusted Bernard and this wife of his. They will rise up and demand that Bishop be released. They will reject this proposal of joint-leadership."

Comrade was vindicated when the people, beginning with the schoolchildren, rose up. On the morning of October 19th they rose up *en masse*, shutting down government installations, including the airport at Pearls, and pouring into St. George's from all corners of the country, some marching on foot, some arriving on the vehicular transport they had commandeered.

They could not imagine the revolution without Maurice Bishop as its sole leader. It was

Bishop's charisma that had given the revolution its legitimacy in their eyes and in the eyes of many people in the wider Caribbean and the world ever since it was proclaimed on the morning of March 13th, 1979 when Comrade, then known by his baptismal name Leroi, was eighteen.

PART TWO

CHAPTER 5

February, 1968

BACK in those days Leroi had not even heard the words 'comrade' and 'dialectics', though later he would answer to the name Comrade and refer to David as Dialectics. David was always different from anyone Leroi knew. No one thought like David, no one read as much or was as knowledgeable. David had dropped his surname, Ollivier, and told Leroi that he was now to be known as David X. The X stood for his surname, which he rejected as a slave master's name and as a badge of shame. He explained to Leroi that he had replaced it with an X as Malcolm Little had done by renaming himself Malcolm X. David claimed that Malcolm X's mother was from Grenada and that he knew the family.

David was a brown-skinned young man of middle height. He wore a black beret, trying to make himself look like Che Guevara. "Che Guevara was the quintessential revolutionary," he told Leroi. He gave Leroi a pin badge of Che Guevara and told him all about this hero of Latin American revolutions.

David was much older than Leroi, but Leroi knew David's parents. They were Miss Bertha and Mister Bertie. They lived by the junction at the other end of the village from Leroi's parents' home. They owned a business that was divided into a grocery shop and a bar or rumshop. David described them, distastefully, as *petit bourseour,* a term Leroi had never heard before and did not understand. Whenever he had money, Leroi would go to the shop to buy the coconut tarts, groundnut sugarcakes, bread and buns that were displayed in a glass case on the counter, or the lollipops in a bottle on the shelf, or snow ice from the fridge. Sometimes he would see David.

He had heard that David was studying at the University of the West Indies at the St. Augustine Campus in Trinidad. Whenever he came home on vacation David would get involved in the radical youth movements that were opposed to the government of Eric Gairy. He would hear from his father that David was beaten and arrested for his anti-government activities and that the government was considering withdrawing his scholarship. He regarded David with awe and was excited the day that David leaned over the counter to hand him the guava cheese he had purchased from the glass case and asked him,

"What's your name, my little friend?"

Leroi gave his full name.

"Pascal... Are you that inspector of police son?"

"Yes." Leroy told him.

"Clarissa is your cousin?"

Leroi confirmed that Clarissa was his cousin. She was like a big sister to him and was very fond of him and he of her. They lived in adjoining yards. She was tall, and her skin was dark brown like a cocoa pod and smooth as a ripe mango. When she pushed him on the swing she made from rope tied to the low branches of a tamarind tree he noticed the growing fullness of her breasts, and saw them jiggling as he sat on a river stone and waited as she washed the laundry or bathed. She took him everywhere with her and when she cooked he was the first to sample whatever she cooked—the oildown, the rice and peas, the dumpling and peas, the pumpkin soup, the fish broth, the pelau, the one-pot, the stew chicken, the callaloo soup, the coo-coo. She was the only child of his uncle Anthony and aunty Madge, or Tanty, as he called her.

The big boys liked Clarissa and, as Leroi was close to her, bribed him with ripe bananas, joints of sugar cane, pennies, wooden tops and marbles to take errands to her from them. She dismissed all of them and told him she liked only David. David was handsome and he was intelligent and ambitious, unlike those other boys who had dropped out of primary school to sit all day on the bridge at the junction and smoke weed, trouble girls, have cookouts in the bush, hunt manicou and fish in the river, drink rum, go to the movies and steal other people's fowls, mangoes, canes and coconuts.

David wanted to be the first boy of the village to attend university. He wanted to study economics. Economics to him was the king of all courses. He also liked history and said he would combine the two. Clarissa was enamoured with him. She said he was well-read and articulate, that he knew how to talk to a girl and that words did not fail him like they failed the other boys.

Leroi had read Clarissa's Mills and Boons paperback books and her comic books that featured teenagers kissing and necking, and he wondered whether Clarissa kissed and necked with boys. He concluded that she would only do it with David, whom she adored. One day he would grow up and would have a girl of his own, one who would love him and who he would kiss and neck with as the boys in the comic books and the Mills and Boons books did. Now David was asking him about Clarissa.

"Tell her to meet me under the cocoa at seven this evening."

Leroi told her: "David say to meet him under the cocoa when it get dark."

She made Leroi promise not to tell anyone about David's message, especially her mother and father.

"I go give you money to buy all the bread and butter, guava cheese, lollipop, cake and snow ice, and the other goodies you like," she promised.

Leroi accepted the deal. It delighted him, but he wondered why David wanted to meet his cousin under the cocoa after dark.

A field of cocoa separated Clarissa's yard from Leroi's grandmother's. Most families in the village owned small cocoa fields. They sold the cocoa beans to the cocoa board which exported it and used the rest to make cocoa loaves and cocoa balls for their own consumption. The cocoa trees were planted close together and their branches often interlocked, blocking out sunlight.

'Under the cocoa' was a reference to being in the cocoa field, under the interlocking branches. The ground under the branches was usually free of undergrowth and covered with a carpet of dried cocoa leaves. Children loved to play under the cocoa during the day, for it was shady and cool and hid them from adults. Adults liked playing their own games under the cocoa at night, because it offered them privacy. Children knew this.

That evening Leroi shadowed Clarissa to the cocoa field and saw her and David meet in an embrace on the path that led to the field. They disengaged quickly and hurried into the cocoa, bending double to avoid the low hanging branches. Leroi followed after them and discovered them lying on the ground on a bed of dry cocoa leaves. Clarissa was looking up into the interlocked cocoa branches at the patches of night sky lit by the moon. David was lying on top of her; Clarissa was moaning, David was grunting, both of them moving together in a brutal rhythm. Leroi retreated in haste. He knew what they were doing.

Children called it 'booming' or 'doing thing'. 'Thing' referred to the unmentionable, the activity that was forbidden to children and involved the male and female genitals. It was the privilege of adults and one could be beaten by adults if one uttered its name. That was why Clarissa had made him promise not to tell her father or mother that she was meeting David under the cocoa—for couples met under the cocoa at night or in the evening to do one thing and one thing alone: 'rudeness', another name children used to refer to the forbidden act.

Leroi knew the consequences of 'doing thing'—children; babies. He and his playmates simulated it all the time with the girls of the neighbourhood, playing house, playing mammy and daddy, playing little popo. Should he tell her parents what his cousin was doing under the cocoa with David, the neighbour's boy?

He was shocked when the following day, David asked him: "Why you mako-ing us?"

How did he know? To mako was to peep and peeping was a vice that was universally

47

disapproved. To be accused of being a mako was a shameful thing—a low-down shameful thing.

"Don't tell anybody what you saw," David made him promise.

"Not if I getting free tart, free snow ice, free cake, free guava cheese, free groundnut sugar cake, free tamarind balls." Leroi replied.

David promised him all these things.

Leroi became David's errand boy, the liaison between him and Clarissa. When they were not meeting under the cocoa, they rendezvoused on the beach, or on the pasture, or behind David's parents' house or in the canefield.

Leroi prayed for the day when he would grow up and enjoy the privilege of 'doing thing' with girls. Boys who had defied authority and experienced the act of 'doing thing' with a girl had said that there was nothing sweeter than *san san*. *San san* referred to the female genitals. Girls had *san san*, boys had *kukus* or *toti*. These were considered obscene words and Leroi wondered why. He wondered whether they were considered obscene just because they were not part of the English vocabulary. When you became a man your toti became big and heavy and when you peed your pee frothed, the boys all agreed. Leroi could not wait to become a man.

His friend Joe John, who was shorter than he was, darker than he was, and 'duncer' than he was but was more handsome, and boasted that his toti had begun to feel longer and heavier, and that when he peed his pee frothed. Joe John was 'friending' with a girl called Margaret who was as precocious as he and who allowed him to feel her budding breasts, kiss their nipples and touch her san san. She had even showed it to him once and he had showed her his toti and allowed her to heft it. Soon, they would be doing thing under the cocoa like the big boys and girls—like the adults.

Joe John was an only child; an only child of his mother, at least. His mother was a seamstress. His father had migrated to the United States and lived in New York. Joe John said he had married a woman who was a citizen 'for stay', meaning that the marriage was bogus—a mere convenience to allow him to regularize his status, become a legal immigrant, acquire residential status, and get a green card. He wrote to Joe John's mother and sent money. He promised to file for Joe John once he became a citizen, so Joe John expected to one day become a U.S. citizen and live in

Brooklyn and marry Margaret, and by marrying her win the approval of the whole world and God to do rudeness with her.

Joe John's father wrote to Joe John's mother that he was alarmed by news that the youths of the country were being radicalized by older youths and young men who had been studying overseas. He asked her to protect their son from such youths. Joe John did not think that he needed protection. He was a big man now. He could think for himself and make his own decisions. His toti was growing larger, feeling heavier, and his pee was making froth. He would soon be 'doing thing' with girls and making them pregnant.

CHAPTER **6**

ONE evening David and a dark, stocky fellow he was hanging out with at the back of his parents' rumshop called Leroi and Joe John to join them. Leroi was holding a copy of the *Gulag Archipelago* in his hand. The stocky fellow snatched it away and threw it in the bush.

"Don't read this stuff," he said sternly. "It would prejudice your mind against communism and reduce you to a lumpen."

A lumpen? It was the first time Leroi had heard the word and it was not to be the last, and it was uttered only by this same fellow.

Some time later Leroi and Joe John were arguing over who had murdered the most people—whether it was Hitler or Stalin. Leroi was arguing that Stalin had murdered more people than Hitler when the fellow came upon them and shouted "lumpen!" at Leroi for besmirching Stalin's reputation. Joe John asked him what 'lumpen' meant.

51

"Short for lumpen proletariat," he said, "lumpen proletariats are low-down people who do not understand the class struggle and their own exploitation."

So Leroi and Joe John nicknamed him Lumpen, without ever knowing his real name.

That was also the first time Leroi had heard the word 'proletariat' and wanted to know what it meant. Lumpen told them that they needed an education and that he would be happy to do the job. In return he asked them if they had any sisters. Neither boy had a sister and Lumpen was very disappointed. Leroi told him he had a cousin named Clarissa, but regretted that David was already on to her. Joe John told him that he was liking a girl named Margaret who had an older sister whom he would gladly introduce him to. Lumpen was happy and said he couldn't wait to meet her.

Lumpen, like David, was a member of the New JEWEL Movement, an organisation which David told Leroi he should aspire to join, since it was almost illegal to be a supporter of it because it defied the authority of the government. It was radical and had openly tried an English Lord called Brunlow who had erected a gate across a path used for centuries by the people, thereby denying them access to a beach called La Sargesse in the south of the island. David had attended the public trial held *in absentia* of the arrogant Lord, and was among those who broke down the gate when the Lord was found guilty on all counts and the people liberated the beach.

Both boys had longed to join the New JEWEL Movement after learning of this incident, of this daring. They had heard that the NJM illegally published and distributed an underground paper. They had never seen it and knew that they could get into trouble if they were caught in possession of it. It had to be read in secret. It was a challenge then to possess it and to read it. David and Lumpen were reading this very paper, and for this Joe John and Leroi regarded them as daring and privileged.

The JEWEL paper was about five pages stapled together. The pages were blotched with black ink from a Gestetner machine and poorly typed on cheap paper. They were illustrated with crude drawings in ink and one of the drawings depicted the prime minister as Lucifer with horns growing out of his head. No wonder it was illegal to be in possession of it. David and

Lumpen had several packets of this paper sitting on the ground between them. David handed a packet to Joe John and another to Leroi.

"You little comrades will deliver these papers for us," he said, "you know the neighbourhood and you like adventure. From now on you involved in something big and dangerous. You understand? You like danger don't you? You like adventure! You like being involved in something big?"

Joe John and Leroi admitted that they liked danger and adventure and relished being involved in something big.

"Good. This very afternoon, you've chosen to become men."

Joe John and Leroi said that they were happy to have become men.

"Then you must act like men and think like men... real men. You must keep this a secret. You must exercise responsibility and do not allow this paper to get into the hands of those it must be hidden from. You must never reveal the identity of those you deliver this paper to."

They promised to be secretive and responsible.

"Don't let your father see this," David warned Leroi, "hide it from him. Give one to Miss Clara, give one to Crebo, give one to Elfi, give one to Franki and give one to Claudette."

That was how Leroi became a distributor of the JEWEL paper without the knowledge of his father. Clarissa knew about it and told him:

"Your father will kill you if he find out. Keep my secret and I'll keep yours!"

She stopped supplying him with her pennies and ten cents and quarters to buy his coconut tarts and cakes and guava cheese and snow ice.

CHAPTER 7

LEROI knew his cousin was in trouble the Saturday morning he went over expecting her to feed him bakes, saltfish and cocoa tea. He found her vomiting behind the kitchen and noticed her parents observing her. When she was through her father shouted at her:

"What's the matter with you, child? Why you having this sickness every morning? Every morning you wake up you have nausea. What's going on with you?"

Clarissa shook her head and said, "I don't know, Daddy!"

Her mother said, "Child, when last you see your period?"

Leroi understood what 'period' was. It was a thing that happened to girls. Clarissa began to stutter and her mother said, "Let's go inside and talk. We need to talk."

They headed for the house and Clarissa's father said to Leroi:

"Not you. Stay outside. This is for family only and even if you were her brother this talk don't concern little boys."

Leroi lingered under an open window of the living room. Suddenly, he heard Clarissa's father bellow:

"What? Tell me who is the boy or man responsible for this. I killing him, so help me God! Where is me cutlass?"

Clarissa's mother was weeping.

"You let me down," she sobbed. "I warn you about boys ever since you had your first period. I warn you about taking man! You still in school. Now you making child and will have to leave before finishing."

Leroi frowned. *Taking man?* He thought. That meant doing thing with men or boys. *Making child?* That meant the girl was pregnant and pregnancy came about from doing thing. Clarissa was in trouble. She would have to drop out of school. It was a pity, for she was in form five, the last form in secondary school, and was preparing for the Cambridge External Exams from England. It was also unfair, for David had finished secondary school without getting pregnant and was now studying at university.

Leroi marched inside his uncle's house.

"What you want?" his uncle bellowed. "I told you to stay outside. You too damn fass!"

"I know who Clarissa making child for," Leroi heard himself saying.

Clarissa was sobbing in a corner. She looked at him and nodded.

"Tell them, Leroi! Tell them!"

"Who she making child for?" Clarissa's father demanded, glaring at Leroi.

"For David, Miss Bertha son," Leroi said and added, "they does do rudeness under the cocoa."

Clarissa's father snorted like an angry bull.

"Where is me cutlass? I going over there for his arse. Planass go pass!"

Leroi knew what a planass was. It was a lash with the flat side of a cutlass, often across the shoulders or on the buttocks. He had never been planassed, but understood that it was painful. He felt sorry for David.

Clarissa's mother cried, "Don't bother, Tony. The boy not at home. He in university over in Trinidad. Wait till he come on vacation."

Clarissa's father didn't wait. He grabbed his cutlass and went over to David's parents' rumshop. By the time Leroi got there, there was a shouting match between David's parents and Clarissa's father. David's father was brandishing his own cutlass and threatening to give Clarissa's father "a good planass in you arse!"

The rum drinkers who had been in the shop put peace between them and tempers cooled.

In the days that followed, Leroi visited Clarissa often. She was miserable. Her mother refused to talk to her and her father insulted her every time he looked at her. At one time Leroi heard him mutter under his breath, but loud enough for Clarissa to hear him: "Taking man instead of studying your books!"

One afternoon Leroi heard a commotion and left Clarissa's side to see what it was all about. He was surprised and alarmed to see David striding towards Clarissa's yard. His parents followed closely behind him. His father was silent and carried a cutlass. His mother wailed and pleaded with David:

"Come back son! Don't go there! That man going kill you and your father going to kill him. Listen to me, son!"

David strode right into the yard and upon

seeing him Clarissa wailed and warned him, "Don't come! Go back! Run, David, run!"

Clarissa's father grabbed his cutlass and brandished it.

"Bastard!" he bellowed, "How dare you come in me yard? Don't come in me yard! I go planass you arse!"

"I come in peace, Sir," David said. "I'm sorry about what happened. I understand your outrage. I accept responsibility. I wish to support Clarissa. I love her very much."

Clarissa's mother was leaning out of a window.

"Come inside," she called. "All you come inside leh we talk! Tony put away that cutlass. Bertie put away that cutlass. We are civilized people. Let's reason with one another."

They accepted the invitation and went inside—David, his parents, Clarissa and her father. Clarissa's father glared at Leroi as he was about to enter the house.

"Go back," he commanded. "Get out of here. You too fass! I say you too fass!"

Leroi lingered in the yard until the meeting was over. There had been no shouting, although he had heard Clarissa sobbing. Clarissa left with David and his parents. She carried a small suitcase and Leroi supposed it contained her clothes.

"Yes, go with them," her unforgiving father shouted at the weeping girl. "I don't want no daughter making child in me house!"

Clarissa went to stay with David's parents. She sometimes served in the shop and Leroi spent most of his time there, feasting on free guava cheese, coconut tarts, groundnut cakes and snow ice.

Three weeks later on a cool, sunny afternoon Clarissa was plaiting David's hair in corn rows under a dwarf coconut tree in the backyard and Leroi was loitering around them eating a half-ripe mango. David said:

"I'm thinking of dropping out of university."

"What?" Clarissa sounded scandalized. "Thinking of dropping out? Why you thinking that? You have to finish your studies, get your degree and come back and get a good job and take care of your baby. Don't forget you about to become a father!"

"Even if I get the degree there is no guarantee I would get a job," David said. "The government is not creating jobs and it's not what you know, not whether you have the necessary academic qualification, the training and experience. It's who you know and whether you are the son of Mr. This or Mr. That in high society and whether your parents support the government or not. I've been an anti-government activist since my secondary school days. The government is unforgiving and has a long memory."

"Oh, David!" Clarissa said. "Sometimes you think too negative!"

"Sometimes I feel that all my efforts are futile," David said. "I'm a politically conscious young man. I see things differently from others. I cannot tolerate injustice. I get into trouble with the university heads and the Trinidad police. I organize protests, I participate in demonstrations. I may not graduate."

"You better graduate." Clarissa said. "Go back and finish your studies. Do your final exams and graduate. Once I have this child I going to study privately for my Cambridge exams."

"Oh, good to hear that!" David cried. "I'll support you. I'll help you study."

CHAPTER 8

November, 1969

DAVID had returned to Trinidad and his studies after his vacation.

"This time he not taking part in no demonstration or getting involve in politics," Leroi's father said to him one night as they sat side by side on the exposed root of an old breadfruit tree in the front yard under a starry sky. "His whole attention is devoted to that girl he got pregnant, your cousin Clarissa. I knew he would get her into trouble. I used to see them sneaking under the cocoa to do thing or creeping under the sea grapes down on the bay. I warn you about that boy. He is trouble."

"But he is bright, Baba," Leroi protested. "He knows a lot of things. He teach me a lot of things and lend me books to read. He encourage me to study my school work and start thinking of going to university. I like him. He love Clarissa and is very good to her. He is not a bad boy."

"He follow bad company and they put a lot of

crazy ideas in his head."

"Don't believe everything you hear about people, Baba," Leroi admonished his father. "I don't believe everything I hear people say about you!"

"Like what?" his father demanded. "What do people say?"

"That you are a bad police, that you beat up people and torture them, especially people who oppose the government, even students. Are you a bad police, Baba? Do you beat people and torture people?"

"Don't believe everything you hear son!"

"Why people fear you?"

"They must fear me. I want them to fear me. I'm a good police. I don't make joke. When I catch the little criminals I bust lash in their tail and throw them in a cell and feed them on bread and water. When they get out they never commit crime again. They always remember the beating and the bread and water. I don't joke with criminals."

"Sometimes I feel shame when I hear of evil things you do, Baba."

"Alleged evil things! You must be proud of your father, son. I enforce the law. You are my only child and I love you as I love myself."

"I believe you, Baba, but you must calm down on the beating and the badness."

"Stay away from David," his father said.

Leroi made no commitment. Nothing could convince him that David was a bad influence. Unlike the other boys, David did not drop out of school, refuse to learn a trade or get a job and lay around all day playing cards or dominoes, hissing at girls, and 'thieving' people's fowl to cook. David had done well in his Cambridge exams, had gone on to excel at his 'A' levels and had been admitted to the University of the West Indies, the first boy of the village to do so.

Leroi's grandmother was very proud of David and continued to admire him even after the scandal involving Clarissa.

"Look how he stood by her side and accept responsibility like a real man, a gentleman!" she said.

Leroi understood the reason for her admiration of David. The other boys would most likely have denied they had anything to do with the girl, might have refused to claim the child as theirs and refused to contribute towards its maintenance, but David had acted as a mature and intelligent man and had remained loyal to Clarissa and true to himself. If Grangran approved of David, Leroi reasoned, there was nothing wrong with being David's friend, despite the disapproval of his father.

Leroi made himself available to Clarissa for most of the day, running errands for her, going to fetch for her the bits of chalk cliff by the river which she craved. Sometimes she allowed him to lay his hand on her swollen stomach and feel the foetus kicking or press his ear to it to hear the baby's heartbeat.

March, 1970

On the day that David arrived for his easter vacation, Miss Bertha called Leroi from where he was playing on the ground with his marbles and asked him to run go and call the village midwife. It was around midday and Miss Bertha told him to tell the nurse that Clarissa's waterbag had burst. Leroi delivered the message faithfully and quickly, and came running back with the elderly midwife. That was when he encountered David entering the yard after the taxi had dropped him off.

"Clarissa making the baby now!" he gasped, and David dropped his suitcase and ran into the house. Leroi ran in after him, but Miss Bertha shooed him away.

"Where you going? What you want?"

"I want to see!"

"See what? What is there to see? Little boy you too fass!"

So Leroi contented himself with pacing about under the window of Clarissa's room, listening to Clarissa huffing and puffing and shrieking in labour, and the midwife encouraging her every now and then to "Push! Push!"

After a while Leroi heard the cry of a newborn baby and Miss Bertha shouting with joy:

"Is a girl! A girl! Me son have a girlchild! I have a granddaughter!"

With bird speed, Leroi took off. He charged into Clarissa's parents' yard, shouting,

"Tanty, Tanty, Clarissa make the child! Is a girlchild!"

Clarissa's mother was happy to hear the news and hurried over to Miss Bertha's.

"Thank you! I glad you fass!" she told Leroi.

On the fifth day Clarissa's mother succeeded

in persuading Clarissa's father to go and see Clarissa and the baby.

When Mr. Bertie saw him, he challenged him:

"Mister man, what you doing in me yard?"

"I come to see me grandchild and take me daughter home." Clarissa's father said.

And so it was that Clarissa and her newborn baby returned to her parents' home. All was forgiven, and David was allowed to visit them freely.

CHAPTER 9

April, 1970

IT was a very volatile time, and there was a lot that excited and confused Leroi. There was a state of emergency in the neighbouring island of Trinidad and Leroi did not understand what it meant. It was all over the radio. One Sunday evening he sat with his grandmother and listened to the premier, Eric Gairy, as he spoke about 'this black power thing'. Gairy began:

> <<*There has been quite some talk recently throughout the region about Black Power...*>>

Leroi was hoping that Gairy would define the meaning of Black Power and his grandmother was hoping the same thing, but Gairy confessed that he was definitely not in a position to criticize the 'Black Power' philosophy or support it, as he did not know too much about it. He knew, however, that:

> <<*In Grenada here, there is no situation that calls*

for, or warrants any Black Power Movement.>>

Leroi's grandmother agreed with Gairy.

"If Uncle says so is so," she said. She nodded in agreement as he said:

<<*Unlike the United States, power is in the hands of the Blacks. Our governor is black, our premier is black, our chief justice is black, our bishop is black. I see the black man in exaltation—in law, in religion, in medicine, in engineering, in economics, in education, in sports, in music and in every field of endeavour.*>>

Granny poked Leroi in the chest and said,

"Pay attention, child. Listen carefully and don't let anyone full up your head with this Black Power nonsense. Uncle won Black Power for us long time ago already."

As if to confirm what she said, Gairy continued:

<<*In 1950-51, I advocated for what could be called power for the Blacks—power to eat and drink like a human being, power to wear clothes like anyone else, power to be given the respect and dignity attributable, as of right, to every human being, the power to be given justice, the power to extend the black man's education in*

quantity and quality and the power to govern our land and people. That was in 1951.>>

His grandmother said: "You hear that, boy? You listening? You paying attention? Uncle won Black Power for us since before you were born. What Black Power those half-educated young people talking about? You stay away from them, you hear?"

Leroi knew that Gairy was including his grandmother when he said:

<<*The very large majority of Grenadians, with a sense of duty and responsibility, will not hesitate, I know, to lend unrelenting and unstinting support to our government in its planned and calculated action to maintain the atmosphere of peace and quiet and law and order, without fear or hindrance.*>>

Leroi gasped as Gairy referred to the disturbances in Trinidad that had occasioned a state of emergency there.

<<*I cannot boast of having the patience of Dr. Eric Williams. It is said that when your neighbour's house is on fire, keep on wetting your own house. We are now doubling the strength of our police force, we are getting in*

almost unlimited supplies of new and modern equipment.>>

Leroi's grandmother shouted, "Hurray!" She shouted hurray again when Gairy said:

<<*My government will not sit by and allow individuals or groups of individuals to agitate or incite, to promulgate or to promote any racial disharmony in this peaceful isle of spice—the Caribbean Garden of Eden.>>*

She sobered up and gasped, "What's wrong with Uncle Gairy?" when he declared:

<<*The opposition to my recruiting criminals in a reserve force. To this I shall not say yea or nay. Does it not take steel to cut steel? I am proud of the ready response to my call on Grenadians, regardless of their record, to come and join in the defense of my government and in the maintenance of law and order in their country. Indeed, hundreds have come and some of the toughest and roughest roughnecks have been recruited. Every man engaged in any form of subversive activity is being watched.>>*

"Toughest and roughest roughnecks!? Uncle Gairy mad?" Leroi's granny exclaimed.

Leroi was trying to make sense of the threat

when Gairy said something else that caught his attention as he continued his speech:

<<*The white-skin lawyer from St. Paul's who once called me a black so-and-so, and who claimed he was white 19 or 20 years ago when we were trying to give the black man some form of recognition, is today, 20 years later, trying to preach 'Black Power'. It took him 20 years of my teaching to make him realize that he is not white. The Black Power Movement is fraught with hypocrisy, false political ambitions, venom and malice.*>>

Leroi wondered who he was referring to. Who was that lawyer who used to play white and was claiming to be black now that some things had changed? Then Gairy said something else that interested him:

<<*If Grenada wants any power at all today, it is certainly not Black Power; it is work power for the very few who are unemployed; money power to meet the cost and standard of living and brain power, more brain power for our youth, so they would become more qualified to hold responsible positions in our state. We cannot eat, drink nor wear Black Power.*>>

Leroi's granny agreed wholeheartedly. The

next day she went into her garden and selected the biggest pumpkin, the biggest bunch of plantains and the choicest mangoes to send them off to Gairy. She always sent Gairy the best of the harvest of her labours—the biggest yams, the biggest sweet potatoes, the choicest Julie mango, mango Ceylon and mango Calcutta, Gairy's favourite mangoes. When sapodilla was in season she sent him sapodillas.

As far as she was concerned, Papa God had sent Gairy and anointed him to lead. Now these crazy youths were threatening his rule with their talk of black power which he had already established since the early fifties.

CHAPTER 10

August, 1971

PEOPLE were pointing their fingers at David and accusing him of 'this black power thing', saying that he was bringing black power to the island.

One day, Leroi's father arrested David for organizing students of a secondary school in Town, that is, in St. George's, where he had gotten a vacation job teaching Social Studies. David was beaten very badly by the police. There was a rumour that his head had been forced into a dirty toilet bowl and the bowl was flushed. Leroi concluded that these roughnecks were really rough and also wondered what they were doing in the police force, and wondered whether his father, an Inspector of Police, was involved. When he did learn that his father was involved in these brutalities, he was mortified.

One day after David was released from the hospital or the prison or wherever he had been, Leroi found him sitting under a long mango tree in his parents' yard, rocking his baby girl. Leroi asked him about his involvement in the Black Power movement and whether it was true that he was not returning to university.

"I'm not going back," he said, "I finish my studies. They could withhold my degree if they want. I'm not attending their graduation ceremony. I'll turn to farming or fishing if I have to if the government deny me a job and try to prevent me from taking care of my woman and my child. I will not stop being an activist until the revolution."

"Revolution? You planning a revolution?" Leroi said.

"A revolution is inevitable with the kind of oppression we under. There is corruption, nepotism, police brutality, and rigged elections. This government must be overthrown. But don't tell your father I say that!"

Leroi promised not to tell.

"Is true they force your head in a toilet bowl and flush the toilet?" Leroi queried.

"Yes, is true. Your father did this to me."

"*My* father?" Leroi found it hard to believe that his father would do such a thing.

"The toilet bowl was full of shit and it stank.

The police in Trinidad did worse to me. They even accused me of being a guerilla. They label young men like me guerilla in Trinidad and shoot them down like dogs and all because our generation is trying to understand the predicaments of our people and discover our mission."

"Which is?"

"To find the solution to these predicaments. That's our mission—the mission of my generation, the mission of your generation. Every generation must discover its mission and either fulfill it or betray it."

"What will yours do?"

"Hopefully fulfill our mission. No generation would like to betray their mission."

"Where did you discover the mission of your generation?"

"At university. At St. Augustine. But they didn't teach us this. They wouldn't imagine doing so. They'd rather hide it from us. Left to the university, we would never have discovered that we had a mission to fulfill."

"Or betray."

"That's not an option that I countenance," David said.

"Tell me about St. Augustine and how you

arrived at your consciousness."

"We were being taught the ideas of Hobbes and Locke, Durkheim and Max Weber, the difficult novels of James Joyce and the debate over whether the sugar industry was profitable or not profitable in the late eighteenth century while so much exciting things are happening all over the world."

"What is happening all over the world?"

"Generations all over the world have discovered their mission and are either fulfilling it or betraying it. Liberation struggles are being waged all over Africa, Latin America and Asia. The whole world is in upheaval over equality, justice and freedom. The cold war is on and affecting the direction and outcomes of those struggles. The civil rights movement is raging in the United States of America and we were learning from sources outside the university about the Russian revolution, the Chinese revolution, the Cuban revolution, the war in Vietnam."

"That sounds interesting."

"We were learning about struggle, about self-knowledge, about self-respect, about revolution. Outside the curriculum, we were reading CLR

James' *Black Jacobins* about the triumph of the Haitian Revolution, the only successful slave uprising in recorded history; we were reading Frantz Fanon's *Wretched of the Earth*, which taught us that each generation must discover its mission and inspired us to discover ours."

"I hope I get to read that book one day."

"We were reading Malcolm X's autobiography and listening to his speeches on tape recorders. We were studying images of white riot police in America attacking non-violent black civil rights marchers with live bullets, batons, police dogs and water hoses and defiant gun-toting black panthers defending their communities. We wanted to be like the panthers. We wanted excitement. We visited the original home of Stokely Carmichael in Oxford Street, shouting his rallying cry of 'Black Power'."

"Who is Stokely Carmichael?"

"A Trinidadian. A conscious brother. A fearless student leader in America. He migrated to America and became a student leader there against white racism. We condemned the fact that he is banned in his own native country as if he is some kind of criminal, as if to oppose racial discrimination and injustice is a criminal offence."

"I sorry to hear that."

"We were urged to act by the ideas, radical ideas, swirling all around us, present in the very air we breathed. The whole world is in upheaval for equality, justice and freedom and we were caught up in this global upheaval."

"How caught up?"

"I was a leader of the students' guild, led by Geddes Granger, the Makandal Daaga you hear so much about in the news. We invited progressive grassroots leaders to lecture to the students. I was an avid organizer of rallies and a leader and instigator of street protests."

"How you manage to attend class and to study?"

"I made time. Throughout this turmoil I completed my final exams and returned to Grenada the day after a state of emergency was declared, for I was forewarned by a police friend that I was marked for death, that I was to be declared a guerilla and killed in cold blood on the pretext that I was armed and opened fire first."

"You were lucky."

"Yes. I was lucky, but when I landed here

police were waiting for me at the airport. Your father the Inspector told me: *'Why you come back here, boy? We doh want you here. You hot and sweaty youths not welcome with your stupid black power nonsense. You in trouble boy. You are a threat to the government and the stability and peace of this country. You should ha' stay in Trinidad for prime minister Eric Williams and police commissioner Burrows to take care of you as they will take care of Daaga and the other black power advocates and guerrillas. You come back to the wrong place. Uncle Gairy is not a joker and we the police are even less tolerant of misguided youths like you. You ever got beaten with a bull pizzle? Trinidad police have bull pizzle? Police in Trinidad too soft. They should ha' sent you back to us in a coffin. We send you to study and get a degree, not to become a radical and turn guerrilla. You in a lot of trouble, boy'.*

"Luckily for me, your father knows my parents. He called the other police aside and spoke to them, then he called me aside and told me: *'You are Bertie's son. I know you. We are neighbours. We from the same village. We may even be related. You were always a bright little boy and the whole village was proud of you when you got accepted in the university, the first boy of the village to go to university. You follow bad company and get caught up in this black power thing and in radical politics. Now you come back I don't want you joining up with we own homegrown black power youths. I don't want you joining the New JEWEL Movement. It is led by radical young men of the brown-skin middle class who just come back from their studies overseas and instead of settling down to their law practice or to teaching the economics and history they qualified in, they determined to remove the government from power because they imagine they know better how to run this country. They are just hot and sweaty youth who think they know all the answers. Stay away from them! Find yourself a job—you can teach or you can join the police force—and keep away from politics! If I ever catch you demonstrating in the street against the government or hanging out with those JEWEL boys I going to take it real personal and break your limbs, not to mention your spirit. I going to show you what black power really is. You see those muscles in my black arm? They contain the real black power. Now you listen to me, boy, and stay away from those people and those situations, stay away from trouble unless you didn't get enough licks from the police in Trinidad. If your body could still take some more all you have to do is cross me and I'll unleash my black power on you. Now go home to your parents, those police officers can't touch you without my permission'. "*

"You should listen to my father. He don't make joke." Leroi advised him.

"No, he don't. A week later I was down in St. George's, in Tanteen area. Some students and teachers were demonstrating against the non-payment of teachers' salaries and I joined the demonstration. Suddenly I felt a stinging lash across my shoulders. My friends told me that I stood stiffly at attention after that first blow. They told me that after the second blow my muscles relaxed and I asked them: *'What was that crack of lightning?'* They told me that after the third blow I asked for snow ice. I remember suddenly feeling thirsty and hot and experiencing a pain so stingingly intense, worse than any pain I had ever suffered before. I turned around and saw your father standing behind me, a formidable bull pizzle in his hand, ready to strike again. I screamed: *'No! What you hitting me for?'*

"Your father shouted at me: '*What you doing in this demonstration, boy? You forget what I tell you? Why you defy me?*' I said: '*I sorry, sah, I was not in the demonstration. I was just standing here in Tanteen, after dropping off an application at Anglican High School and Palmer School when the demonstration overtook me*'. Your father shouted at me again: '*Shut you lying mouth. I'm giving you a second chance. Now go home. Buy a snow cone or a snow ice or drink plenty ice water. Bull pizzle does make people thirsty; it does generate a lot of heat in their body*'.

"That day I ate a lot of snow ice and drank a lot of ice water, but my thirst was unquenchable and the heat inside me would not cool down. I got a job teaching history at the Presentation Boys Secondary School the following week. I guess the sympathetic Catholic priests that run the school took pity on me. I am a past student of that school and they remembered me."

"How come you never listen to my father? You suffer all these arrests and pain. For what?"

"For revolution. I'm a revolutionary. I must make sacrifices. I'm prepared to sacrifice my life in the struggle. I don't listen to your father because he is a reactionary. He represents the forces of reaction. I cannot give in to him."

CHAPTER 11

May, 1972

ONE day a friend brought David to the law offices of Maurice Bishop and Kenrick Radix, his partner and childhood friend, and told them that he wanted to become a member of the New JEWEL Movement. Maurice Bishop was a large man, but gentle. He was tall and fair-skinned, Radix was dark. Maurice Bishop told David that the original Joint Endeavour for Welfare Education and Liberation was a rural St. David's movement and that his own Assemblies of the People, a small urban-based group without a rural base, had merged with JEWEL to form the New JEWEL Movement and that he and Unison Whiteman of JEWEL were joint leaders. They made David a member. Soon after he became a member, his friend introduced him to a study group within the NJM called OREL (Organization for Revolutionary Education and Liberation). David became a member of OREL and participated in its studies.

Leroi was interested in these exploits.

"What do you study?" He inquired of David.

"Political science, Marxist-Leninist ideology. Our main tutor is a Grenadian lecturer at St. Augustine, a brilliant economist called Bernard Coard. He and Maurice Bishop know each other as friends since their student days and share an ambition to become prime minister of Grenada one day."

"Does Bishop know about this OREL study group?"

"Sure. He, Radix and Whiteman and the others know about it. Our conclusions guide NJM. We analyze this whole black power thing and came to the conclusion that the problem we face in this country and region is one of class, not of race or colour. The class analysis was missing from the black power focus on race and colour and as a result it distorted the reality, obscured the real problem and so gave us a warped idea of our predicament.

"The predicament of our people is the mission of our generation to solve. From then on the NJM has become a socialist-oriented movement and since elections are invariably rigged, revolution has become one of our main objectives. The government would have to be forcibly removed, either by popular people's power or by armed insurrection. Since people's power is not working, Gairy simply allow the people to march till they get tired and go home or till he tires of them calling upon him to step down, and then he send his police and thugs to break up their demonstrations. We have decided that the only option left to us is armed struggle."

"Armed struggle?"

"We have a military wing we call the National Liberation Army. It is in training. Many of our members in the Cadet corps undercover. And we're not the only militant group. They have other militant groups in St. Patrick's, in Tivoli and elsewhere."

"Why you telling me all this?"

"Because you are one of us. You distribute our JEWEL papers. I'm going to make you an official member of the New JEWEL Movement."

"My father will kill me!" Leroi was visibly alarmed.

"He will not. You are his son, his only child. He will rant and rave, he may even threaten you or lash you with this bull pizzle of his, but he will not kill you. All over the island politics dividing families. Children joining the radical groups; parents remaining staunch supporters of Gairy and his party and government. Why? We of NJM and OREL understand why. Gairy came at a right time. He understood the predicament of our people in the 1950s. They were under the yoke of the colonial authorities and the exploitative plantation system. He even analyzed the problem correctly as a class problem rather than a race problem, though he acknowledged the important role that race and colour played in the class prejudice that existed at the time. He discovered the mission of his generation at quite a young age."

In 1951 Eric Gairy had started a trade union movement, through which he mobilized and organized the people and offered them his leadership. He brought the country people down to St. George's to demand higher wages and better working conditions on the estates. To the status quo it was the most visible and threatening demonstration of people's power in the history of the island since the abolition of slavery in 1838. The colonial authorities reacted predictably and tactlessly, with brute force, disproportionate force, and violence. There was bloodshed and rioting.

Power concedes nothing without a demand, and soon enough the colonial authorities had to admit defeat and make concessions. One of the concessions they made was universal adult suffrage. Before then, only white men, particularly men with property and a certain amount of cash, could vote. Poor people, who were mostly black, and women, including white women, could not vote. In addition to that concession, the conditions of work on the plantations were improved and wages were raised.

Eric Gairy was revered by the older generation as a hero and liberator. The people exercised their right at every election to vote him into power. That generation understood more than any other generation the importance of the right to vote. Gairy supporters never failed to register to vote and always turned out in large numbers at the polls to vote for him. He could boast that if he sent a lizard or a ground dove to represent him, his people would vote for the lizard or the ground dove.

"That's why my grandmother worships him so," Leroi said, suddenly enlightened. "She say he caused her generation to afford to wear drawers, even though the drawers they wear make from flour bag. She say that at least they no longer go about naked under their skirts and dresses. She says that in the old days, before Gairy, whenever the wind blow up their skirt their business would be exposed to the whole world. She say thanks to Gairy, their modesty is now protected."

"She is right. And we appreciate her gratitude to Gairy. He is, or was, a true hero of the people, a real man of the people."

"Why *was*? Has he betrayed his mission?"

"At first he appeared to have fulfilled it, but he has not stayed the course. He has betrayed his mission. His government corrupt. He practices nepotism, take bribes, panders to the very class which, with their colonial mentality, opposed him in his early days of class struggle, wishing to join their exclusive clubs, sleep with their wives and daughters, share in their profits, live in their exclusive residential areas."

"But your New JEWEL Movement leaders, your Maurice Bishop, for example, come from that same brown-skin upper class. The others almost all from the middle class, from what you tell me, and were born and grow up with privileges people like me and you never enjoyed."

"Yes, Leroi, but they identify with us, the working class. They are grassroots like us. They are for us. They are dedicated to our liberation and upliftment. I'll teach you the science of our party, the ideology that guides us. You'll be my student... I'll be your tutor."

Leroi soon learned that there were other youths who were David's students and official members of the NJM and who, like him, worked for David distributing JEWEL papers to an ever-widening network of supporters. David cautioned them to keep their membership secret, to be wary of government informers whom he identified as secret police and to never disclose the identities of the people who bought the JEWEL papers every week. These people were very important supporters—essential to the survival of the NJM as a movement. They hid the printing machines and the members of the NJM who had reasons to disappear underground from time to time until the pressure on them, mostly from the police, eased.

David and Lumpen tutored them in the back room of his parents' shop, under the cocoa, in the open pasture at nights, on the beach, under the protection of the windswept seagrapes, in the mountains under the cover of a hike, or at a camp-out.

Leroi came to like these activities. They were exciting; they were adventurous; they were forbidden and therefore delightfully daring. He liked the lectures and instructions in political science and ideology, and in Marxist-Lenininst ideology, which David said was the ideology of revolution.

David sounded learned as he expounded on historical materialism, dialectical materialism, the contribution of Hegel, Engels and Marx, the inevitability of class struggle and the inevitable triumph of the working class.

He was fond of uttering the word 'dialectics'. It sounded sticky in his mouth, like chocolate or toffee, or starchy like yam or dasheen. He loved uttering it as one loved eating chocolate or toffee or yam. So Leroi and the other students nicknamed him 'Dialectics'.

CHAPTER **12**

THE little group was broken up when a sexton called Gussie, short for Augustus, discovered that a boy called Joe John was distributing JEWEL papers. Joe John had a curious habit of undressing himself fully when engaged in any bodily function. When at home, he stripped off all his clothes to go to the toilet. If he was away from home and the need to use the toilet possessed him and obliged him to go into the bushes, he did the same thing.

One evening he lured his girlfriend Margaret into the church cemetery. Margaret was content to drop her underwear and lift the hem of her dress above her waist and lay on her back on a cold marble tombstone, but Joe John had to remove his shirt, his shoes, his trousers and his underpants and discard them on the ground before he could lie on top of her to 'do his thing'.

Gussie, the sexton, caught them at it as he was walking home through the cemetery after ringing the church bell. Joe John leapt off Margaret and ran naked out of the cemetery. Margaret took her time, got up off the tombstone, brushed down the skirt that had bunched up around her waist, and walked haughtily away, ignoring Gussie's accusation that she was a bad little girl, a drag-about, which he pronounced 'dragabat', and his threats that he knew her parents and would tell on her and that what she and the boy were doing was disturbing the peace of the dead who had long ago forsaken that kind of activity, which was a vice only of the living and which they did not wish to be reminded of, having departed this life.

Gussie folded up Joe John's clothes and discovered under them a large packet. He opened the packet and discovered the banned JEWEL papers—an edition that depicted government ministers and judges as clowns and labeled Prime Minister Gairy as the 'crime minister' and depicted him as Lucifer with horns growing out of his head. Gussie was incensed. He waited behind a tombstone for the boy to return for his papers and his clothes.

Joe John returned soon enough, bent forward, walking stealthily and looking furtively about him, his hands covering his now shrunken manhood. When he reached his bundle of clothes and packet of JEWEL papers, Gussie nabbed him. At first Joe John thought it was a spirit of the dead and nearly panicked. But it turned out to be the living in the person of Gussie the sexton.

Gussie dragged him, struggling and demanding to be released, to the police station. He was interrogated by Inspector John John. He told Inspector John John that he was a member of the NJM and was one of a network of distributors of JEWEL papers. He identified David as their recruiter, tutor and supplier of the proscribed papers. He identified the receivers of the papers. When the Inspector heard that his son was a member of the NJM and a distributor of its proscribed paper he bellowed:

"What! I'm going to kill that boy! You sure is me boy you talking about? You certain is him? He dead! He damn dead!"

The inspector gave Joe John a lash with his bull pizzle and ordered him to get out of his presence—Go! But Joe John could not move. His muscles were seized and he stood rooted stiffly to the spot, at attention.

"I know what would make you move," the Inspector grumbled, "I know the remedy."

Wap!

The Inspector whet him a second lash with the bull pizzle. Joe John leapt into the air and landed on his feet facing the door. He bolted out of the door like a bullet. He ran howling down the street. He ran into Dialectics.

"Comrade," he panted, "buy a snow ice for me!"

Dialectics asked him where he had been and why he was fleeing and craving snow ice. The craving forced him to confess all to Dialectics. Dialectics bought him a couple of snow ice and commanded him to go and make the rounds, warning all those whose names he had called.

Many of them were rounded up by the police before they could go underground. Dialectics himself escaped to St. Vincent via speedboat from the northern town of Sauteurs.

After three months underground in St. Vincent, Dialectics returned. He, Leroi and Clarissa were at a dance in Birchgrove one Saturday night when the Inspector came up to him and hissed in his ear:

"You little wretch! I have a good mind to arrest you and take you to the police station and reintroduce my bull pizzle to your shoulders, back and bam bam! How dare you recruit me son?"

Leroi begged his father to forgive Dialectics and refrain from harming him.

"He better be on his p's and q's!" the Inspector shouted. "He being watched day and night! His activities being monitored twenty-four-seven! We know what he has for breakfast, when he visits the toilet, the colour of his pee, what lies he tell his girlfriend, how badly he screw her. He is a good boy who means well, but he is with the wrong set of people. He should'ha joined the government if he cares for the people so much. I believe his motivations are genuine, sincere, honorable, but he is the perfect example of the misled leading the unsuspecting and ignorant. The leaders of this NJM he love so much are the children of the big shots who have always resented Gairy. They grew up in homes where they heard their parents and their parents' associates talk with contempt of Gairy, of black-skin people in general and of country people who they dismiss as uneducated and superstitious.

"Read their JEWEL papers carefully and you'd see for yourself the emphasis they place on Gairy's black complexion, the fact that he originated from rural Grenada, from the countryside, and the fact that he not university-educated like them and did not attend any of the prestigious schools in St. George's they attended. This class of people always felt that Gairy is too black, too rural, too uneducated to rule, that they more qualified on the basis of their class, their fairer complexion, their wealth and their education. Forget about all this talk of justice and equality and wanting to get rid of illiteracy, superstition and backwardness. All they want to do is replace Gairy by hook or by crook and monopolize power within their class. They not interested in elections because each time they participate in elections they fail to defeat Uncle Gairy! They then say he rigged the election! Uncle don't have to rig any election. They know that. He has staunch support and his supporters come out to vote in large numbers every time, come rain, come shine, on election day."

He paused for breath, then continued his ranting.

"They wish Uncle Gairy would be a dictator like Batista and Pinochet to justify overthrowing him and they provoke him into becoming one or reacting in ways which would confirm their propaganda that he is a dictator. They are a violent lot! They believe in violence! They want to emulate the Cubans and have an armed struggle and the violent overthrow of the Government. They will do so over my dead body! They have started their assassinations. They have assassinated Inspector Belmar."

The assassination of Inspector Belmar over the Christmas season had alarmed Leroi's grandmother. With tears in her eyes, she had confronted John John.

"Son," she wept, "it don't pay to be bad. Look, Belmar was bad. He was one badass policeman, so bad that a Calypsonian make a calypso on him warning people to beware of this man. Now look what they do to him. They could do it to you too. You have no right to be beating up people and torturing them. I didn't bring you up to behave that way. I don't know where you get this badness from. Stop ill-treating members of the public and abusing your police powers, otherwise you might end up like Belmar."

John John told her not to worry.

"Dem fellas can't touch me. They 'fraid me like cat fraid holy water! Those JEWEL boys assassinate Inspector Belmar. They guilty of it, despite their protestation of innocence. Well, if it's Inspectors of Police they starting with, they better beware of me! You begging me not to harm that boy David, but if I catch him again breaking the law or provoking the government I will do to him what the police in Trinidad forget to do to him or didn't imagine could be done! Those JEWEL boys strategy is to destroy a popular leader's reputation with propaganda, calling him Lucifer, calling him Crime Minister, ridiculing his belief in UFOs, at the same time provoking him into anger and unpopular actions that they then blow out of proportion. Exaggerating everything for local and international consumption, claiming Gairy is a dictator and labeling us police as brutes and brutal for doing our duty of keeping the peace and maintaining law and order.

"When they come and start their nonsense Grenada's economy was no worse than the economy of St. Lucia or St. Vincent or Dominica or Antigua and Gairy was no more a dictator than the chief ministers of those other small islands. These bad-minded fellas set about provoking Gairy, exaggerating conditions and creating their artificial revolutionary condition to justify their planned violent overthrow of the government. And their seizure of power to fulfill their personal and class ambitions. And their belief that only *they* fit to rule and no 'little black boy', as they refer to Gairy, should govern Grenada."

He cautioned Leroi:

"You were wrong to join them and I have a good mind to break your neck, but you're my son, even though I regret the day I parted your mother's thighs so she could conceive you. You have sinned against me. Go and sin no more!"

PART THREE

CHAPTER 13

March 13th, 1979

THE morning of March 13th, 1979 was a calm, sunny morning, as innocent as all other mornings.

As Leroi was preparing for school he turned on the radio to the playing of a calypso by Brother Valentino, supporting the struggle of the native peoples of Rhodesia to free themselves of racist oppression and rename their country Zimbabwe. Brother Valentino sang: *'Stay up Zimbabwe! Stay up Zimbabwe!'*

The song was interrupted by the voice of an unfamiliar announcer saying that the Government of Sir Eric Gairy had been overthrown at dawn by the military arm of the New JEWEL Movement, and calling on ordinary people to welcome the new revolutionary government and seize police stations.

"Oh Papa God!" Leroi's grandmother wailed. "They overthrow Uncle Gairy! This country will never be the same again. They have no idea what they have done. What have they done? What have they done?"

Leroi forgot about going to school and sat down with her.

"Where is your father?" she said. "I hope your father safe. He was an implacable enemy of these JEWEL boys. Now they have seized power. My son is as good as dead."

She began to weep. Leroi hugged her around the shoulders and cooed in her ear.

"Don't cry, Grangran. Baba is alright. There was no bloodshed. They are calling it a bloodless revolution."

He was still comforting and reassuring his grandmother when John John came home. He was grinding his teeth in anger. He spoke to no one. He poured himself a glass of white rum, drank it in one gulp without chasing it with water, and lay on the couch with his boots on.

"Damn JEWEL boys!" he muttered. Then he said to Leroi:

"That friend of yours David, son of Miss Bertha, was involved in the attack of the barracks. Did he tell you of the planned attack?"

"No Baba. I had no idea."

"So he did not confide in you. You know why?

He didn't trust you."

Leroi did not believe this, but said nothing.

Later that morning the leader of the NJM, Maurice Bishop, addressed the nation. It was around half past ten and Leroi had been listening to the radio all morning. He recorded and memorized the speech, conscious of the fact that this was history happening in real time, as David loved to say. John John listened to the broadcast with a sneer on his face. Grangran listened to it with apprehension.

<<At 4:15 this morning, the People's Revolutionary Army seized control of the army barrack at True Blue. The barracks were burned to the ground. After half-an-hour of struggle, the forces of Gairy's army were completely defeated, and surrendered. Every single soldier surrendered and not a single member of the revolutionary forces was injured. At the same time, the radio station was captured without a shot being fired. Shortly after this, several cabinet ministers were captured in their beds by units of the revolutionary army. I am now calling upon the working people, the youth, workers, farmers, fishermen, middle-class people, and women to join our armed revolutionary forces at central positions in your communities and to give them any assistance which they call for.>>

Leroi's favourite part was towards the end of the speech:

> <<*People of Grenada, this revolution is for work, for food, for decent housing and health services, and for a bright future for our children and great-grandchildren.*>>

John John was angry at the end of the speech. He sneered:

"This is not a people's revolution. This is a seizure of power by the JEWEL boys in the name of the people. The people were not consulted and took no part in it."

Dialectics swung into the village at noon in a jeep seized from the Ministry of Fisheries. He was accompanied by boys armed with second World War issue .303 rifles seized from surrendered police stations. Excited by the sight of the guns and the promise of adventure, boys from the village joined what Dialectics referred to as the provisional revolutionary army. Joe John was the first to volunteer.

They went from house to house demanding that residents fly a white flag above their roofs to indicate they had surrendered and that they supported the revolution. Old, torn bedsheets, old blouses, bras and panties went up. John John refused to put up a white flag on the house as an indication that he was not opposed to the revolution.

"I ain't flying no damn flag!" he shouted. "Haul all you little arse outa me yard before I pull me bull pizzle or me cutlass."

"Ha," Dialectics said. "Your government has been overthrown but you still playing bad-john! The revolution will cut you down to size."

Grangran told Leroi:

"Son, never mind him. He is frightened, that's all."

She handed him a piece of white garment.

"Here. Hoist this up on that bamboo pole over there and lean it against the house."

Leroi sniggered when he saw what it was—an old, bleached pair of flour bag drawers.

As they were leaving, Dialectics said to Leroi:

"You coming with us? We have to be vigilant and prepared. There are mercenaries out there. We have to guard our beaches."

Leroi looked at his father and the expression on the man's face was enough to discourage him.

Grangran said:

"Missionaries? Who are these missionaries? Why would they attack us?"

"Not missionaries, Grangran," Leroi said. "Mercenaries."

"Never heard of them," she said.

All through the day open jeeps full of boys and young men holding .303 rifles raced past at full speed, responding to false alarms of mercenaries who had landed on this beach or the next. They all wore white armbands emblazoned with a rising sun, signifying the new dawn that had broken.

Leroi made an armband for himself, but hid it from his father.

"They'll come for you, son," Grangran said to his father. "I hear they picking up known Gairyites. Some of Gairy ministers were arrested early morning in their beds. I hear Richmond Hill prison is full to bursting with detainees."

"Let dem come," John John said defiantly. "Let dem come. I have me bull pizzle and me cutlass ready and I have a pistol full of bullets."

"This is no time to play bad-john, son," Grangran said. "All the other bad-john police have surrendered as well as the members of the mongoose gang—those roughest and toughest roughnecks that Uncle Gairy said in his speech he was recruiting to fight his opponents. I hear that Green Face, Willie, Pram and others have all been rounded up."

It was at this point that an idea occurred to Leroi.

"I know of a way I could protect you, Baba," he said.

His father glared at him. Grangran queried:

"What way, son? What can you do?"

"Join them," Leroi said. "I can join the militia. They will say that the father is against them but at least the son is on their side. I'll know in advance if they planning to arrest Baba and I can plead with them, plead with Dialectics to spare Baba, to forgive him, to have mercy on him. All Baba have to do is behave himself, keep a low profile, keep his mouth shut and keep the flag of surrender flying on the bamboo pole even though it's just one of Grangran's old drawers."

"Hmmmn!" Grangran sighed and said, "you think dat would work?"

"I hear other boys doing it to protect their family." Leroi said.

"Well," John John said, "go and join them, but

be careful how you handle them guns. Those weapons are dangerous and all you young boys have no training in handling them."

Thus encouraged, Leroi hopped on a jeep which had come up to the junction of the village and was turning to go back.

"You joining us?" A tall young man who Leroi recognized as a senior in his secondary school said. "Hop on!"

Leroi sat among boys his age in the jeep. They were all holding .303 rifles.

"I hear that mercenaries are landing on Blue Fish Bay!" A woman shouted.

Off they went speeding toward Blue Fish Bay. Leroi wondered what he would fight the mercenaries with. He was not armed.

CHAPTER 14

THERE were no mercenaries at Blue Fish Bay. The only activity there was a group of fishermen pulling in a seine net that had caught a school of sprats. The boys were disappointed. They drove away and inspected two other bays, but they were also free of mercenaries so they returned to camp.

Camp was an old great house that Dialectics and Lumpen had appropriated to serve as headquarters for their militia. Dialectics had them all lined up in the great yard and those without arms were given their own .303 rifles. Leroi held his awkwardly, finding it heavy. Holding it made him feel brave and invincible, even though he had no idea how to load it and fire it.

"Soldiers of the Provisional Revolutionary Army." Dialectics addressed them. "This is your captain speaking."

Dialectics had been modest enough to acquire for himself the rank of captain. Lumpen had styled himself lieutenant-colonel and preferred to be addressed as colonel.

"This is a popular revolution," Dialectics said. "A true revolution. All over the country people have taken to the streets in celebration and to show their support. A white flag flying from every rooftop. The die-hard Gairyites are the only people who are not supporting us. This morning we received baskets of bakes and freshly baked bread, bowls of saltfish souse and buckets of hot cocoa tea from people providing us with breakfast. They have been coming up here to bring us lunch as well."

Even as he spoke a woman entered the yard with a wooden tray covered with white linen balanced on her head. Lumpen accompanied her inside the house. Leroi got a whiff of oildown, his favourite dish—breadfruit and dumplings, and meat cooked in coconut milk under a covering of dasheen leaves, or callaloo leaves, as they were also called.

"For those of you who just join us, this camp is called Camp Supplice. You may be wondering who is Supplice? Supplice is the name of one of our marron leaders of the old slavery days. He was the leader of a group of runaway slaves who hid in the folds of the mountains and the fastness of the rainforest and raided the plantations and generally made slavery an expensive and risky enterprise for the people who owned and lived in this great house at the time and enslaved our ancestors on their plantation.

"Supplice resisted slavery and enjoyed his freedom as a fugitive till his death. He was never captured. In the spirit of Supplice and others like him we have made this revolution and will defend it. The spirit of Supplice lives in me, it lives in you, it lives in all of us. Supplice has come down from the mountain and taken over the great house. Let's all shout hurray! Hip hip?"

"Hurray!" they shouted in unison.

"Let's go to lunch."

They all trooped into the great house. There was a long table in the middle of the great dining hall and on it was laid out a buffet of the food that people had contributed. There was oildown, rice and peas, stewed fowl, curry goat, boiled ground provisions, callaloo, pea soup with little round dumplings, macaroni pie and fried plantain.

While they were eating the phone rang and Dialectics answered it. He returned and informed the militia:

"There was a report that mercenaries had landed on Sauteurs Bay up in the north, but it was a false alarm put about by counter-revolutionaries and destabilizers."

It was the first time Leroi heard the terms 'counter-revolutionary' and 'destabilizers'.

"Another piece of news," Dialectics said, "and this is not propaganda. A young comrade was killed in Grenville when his .303 went off as he was cleaning it. The bullet blew off his face. Comrades are being killed and wounded from mishandling their .303. I urge you to take precaution and handle these old rifles with care."

After lunch Leroi found Dialectics sitting under a long mango tree, his .303 cradled in his lap.

"I see you've decided to join us, comrade," Dialectics said. "I am surprised that your father allowed you, or are you just being your rebellious self?"

"He allowed me." Leroi said. "He has surrendered. He accept the fact that he has no power to stop this change that has taken place."

"So he is not planning anything?"

"NO." Leroi replied. "He does not wish to cause any trouble. He knows he can no longer continue being an inspector of police because of his past, so he just want to stay at home and work his land, plant his banana, cultivate his cocoa, gather his nutmeg. All he asks is to be left alone."

"Can we leave him alone?" Dialectics said. "Can we ever trust him and people like him? They are potential counter-revolutionaries. I have a good mind to pick him up and put him away."

"Leave him alone!" Leroi pleaded. "He is harmless and people in the village would cry shame on you if you pick him up. All o' we are one family. You related to him and me on your mother side. He has promised to behave himself. He is no fool. He knows when he is beaten. He knows who is now in power. Just leave him alone."

"Alright," Dialectics said. "I'll leave him alone, but I'll be watching him and I'll be listening to him so he better watch his mouth. I'll arrest him and throw him in jail upon the slightest suspicion of counter-revolutionary activity, and if I hear him utter or it is reported that he uttered the slightest thing against the revolution or its leaders."

"I will warn him," Leroi promised. "I will tell him what you say. But I know he would behave himself and spend his time in his garden tending to his corn and peas, his sweet potato and cassava, his yam and his dasheen."

"He better had." Dialectics announced harshly.

That evening the provisional revolutionary army marched through the village on its way to the bay to watch out for mercenaries. The people came out to gawk at them and Leroi saw the envy on the faces of the smaller boys, the admiration in the eyes of the girls and heard the awe in the voices of the older people as they marveled: "Such big guns in the hands of small boys!"

Leroi and Joe John kept guard together on a headland.

Joe John said, "I leaving school for good. I ain' going back. I joining the army. Dialectics say there going be an army. The People's Revolutionary Army. I decide to become a soldier."

"I'll stay in school and attend militia training." Leroi said.

"I go wear a uniform and carry a gun. Women go throw themselves at me." Joe John replied.

The night grew older. They got bored. The stars twinkled above, the waves broke relentlessly, the sea roared. No landing craft slanted to shore, no mercenaries materialized out of the darkness. Joe John shouldered his .303 and fired anyway. The report was loud and the recoil sent Joe John tumbling backwards into the sea. He emerged spluttering, dripping wet and without his .303 as Dialectics, Lumpen and other militia came running to the headland. They had many questions for Joe John and Leroi.

"What's the matter? What happen? Why you open fire?"

"I thought I saw a head break the surface of the water," Joe John said. "I imagine it was a mercenary and open fire on the bastard. Was probably a turtle."

"It probably was," Dialectics said. "There are rumours that mercenaries have landed at la Sargesse and Petit Bacolet in St. David. I'm sure it's not true. Who is spreading those rumours?"

They were relieved by another shift. Leroi spent the rest of the night on a blanket in a second floor room of the old great house, his .303 by his side. The wind moaned in the eaves of the house and the boards creaked and groaned. Shadows fleeted across the glass windows. Despite the gun at his side, Leroi was scared. He had heard that great houses were haunted places—inhabited by the ghosts of previous times. He felt certain that the ghosts of the old slave masters were unhappy that the descendants of those they had enslaved had appropriated their old residence and turned it into a military camp.

"MacAdams, haul your arse!" He heard someone curse aloud.

He understood why. MacAdams was the old owner of the great house and his ghost must have been tormenting the comrade. One of the surest ways to rid oneself of ghosts was to curse them. The more offensive and obscene the language, the better.

"Fuck out of here! Get thee behind me Satan!" The comrade shouted. Leroi wondered whether the comrade was shouting in his sleep or whether he was awake.

The following morning, villagers brought their breakfast in wooden trays, baskets and buckets. There were buckets of cocoa tea, baskets of bakes and freshly baked bread, plates of fried breadfruit and fried plantain, bowls of fried jacks and titiri cakes, mugs of cassava farine. Leroi ate and ate.

When they went out on patrol, adults and children came running out of houses and yards, waving and shouting: "Long live the revolution! Forward ever, backwards never!" Leroi saw for himself that this was a popular revolution.

The following Thursday Dialectics brought the militia to Queen's Park in St. George's participate in the first rally. Tens of thousands of people attended. They came from all corners of the country and from all walks of life. They came for direction. They came to be reassured.

Maurice Bishop, who had been proclaimed as the leader of the revolution, reassured them that general elections would be held within six weeks. Or was it six months? Leroi had forgotten. At the time of the announcement he was outside the pavilion chatting up a pretty girl who was standing beside a woman selling mint, cigarettes and an assortment of other things from a wooden tray. Leroi was boasting to her that he had joined the militia, had held a gun and was committed to defending the revolution.

The woman overheard him and laughed. The girl told him that the woman was her mother. He felt shy and turned away. The woman said to him,

"Don't go, son. Keep on chatting. Check out if you checking out!"

He felt encouraged. Here was a liberal mother. To 'check out' was to woo and she didn't mind him wooing her daughter. Would she mind him doing thing with the girl? He imagined himself doing thing with her. At night. Behind the pavilion or in one of the houses in River Road. The girl had told him she lived with her mother in River Road. Her mother supported the revolution.

He never saw the girl after that day and even forgot her name after a while, but whenever he passed through River Road he looked out for her. He told himself that he was old enough now to have a girlfriend and experience the pleasure of doing thing, though the thought of fatherhood terrified him. Doing thing carried the risk of fatherhood—of parenthood—and he told himself that he was not yet prepared for such responsibility. He was still in school, had not yet grown a beard, his pee had not yet begun to froth. Perhaps the revolution would turn him into a man.

His grandmother had joked that the

revolution would turn a lot of boys and girls into forced-ripe men and women, forced-ripe revolutionaries. He didn't want to be a forced-ripe man or a forced-ripe revolutionary. He wanted to mature naturally. When you picked a green mango or sapodilla or any fruit from the tree and hid it away and its skin turned yellow, it was said to be forced-ripe because you had swaddled it in straw, covered it down, and forced it to ripen.

Leroi returned to school towards the end of March. Many of his male schoolmates had decided not to return. They had joined the army and taken up arms in preference to books. Grangran said to him, "You done the right thing, son." His father said to him, "Guns and books don't mix too well, but you can continue with your militia training so long as you study your books and continue to get good grades and keep an eye on Dialectics. See that he leave me alone."

"Yes, Baba. But you must behave yourself and refrain from criticizing the revolution so much, especially when you drink your rum. I wish you wouldn't drink so much!"

Before the revolution John John never drank, but now that he was no longer an inspector of police he visited Bertie's rumshop every evening and drank until late in the night. He came home drunk, loudly condemning "that bloody revolution" for all his woes.

CHAPTER 15

AS Leroi was leaving for training one evening, his father said to him in a low, conspiratorial tone:

"I hear your leader fancies himself a prime minister like Gairy, with executive power and the freedom to go to the club and drink with his big shot friends and do as he please. But reality going to soon dawn on him that he is not, and cannot be a prime minister like Gairy. True, he has a cabinet, but it's the party that put him in power, and the party could remove him any time. It is the party, the Central Committee of the party, that makes decisions and policies, that tell *him* what to do.

"Gairy was his own man, no one could tell Gairy what to do. So he cannot be no prime minister like Gairy because they destroy the constitution that would have given him the executive power, and besides, he was not elected prime minister by the people. He wants to be, but cannot be a revolutionary leader like Fidel Castro, a charismatic, maximum leader.

"The others wouldn't let him and he don't have the talent and natural authority of Castro, his single-mindedness and energy, his organizational and oratory skills. A friend of mine who is up there with them tell me that one day these issues would create a split in the leadership and that Bishop would lose. You beware, boy!"

Leroi was chastened. Crestfallen, his head bowed, he went to join the fellas sitting on the low bridge by the junction eating sugarcanes stolen from a nearby cane field and talking, not about Hegel and Engel and Marx, whom they had heard Dialectics and Lumpen talk about, or about historical materialism, dialectical materialism and the inevitability of the triumph of the proletariat, but about girls, sports and the latest movies. Fellas boasted about the girls they had taken to the grove of guavas, under the cocoa, to the pasture on a moonlit night, to the beach, behind the cinema, even to the bell tower of the Catholic Church. Like Joe John, fellas had taken girls to the cemetery.

Joe John said that Margaret's cries that *she was coming, she was coming, she was coming, Oh God!* had alerted Gussie, for they were in a part of the cemetery that was well away from the footpath Gussie used as a shortcut. The fellas were amused and accused Leroi of being quiet, of listening to their secrets and not revealing his. Some suspected him of getting more girls than they did; of being silent and not telling. With his reputation of not telling, girls found it easier to give him their favours.

Leroi wished that this was true, and to satisfy the fellas' curiosity and ease the pressure on himself, he told them that he had taken "that girl Charlotte" under the silk cotton tree where he had waited for her as planned as she returned from her Pentecostal church one night. The boys were impressed, but some expressed disbelief— Charlotte?? That good-looking girl, so well brought up, always nicely dressed, with good manners, a born again Christian, "butter can't melt in she mouth?" Charlotte who minded her own business and her school books and bible and had no time for boys, who would not say hello to them and would not turn around and look at them when they hissed at her or peeped at her when she passed?

The fellas considered it a privilege that he had conquered Charlotte and respected him for it. They pestered him with questions: Was she a virgin? Was she tight? Did she squirm and scream? Did she have an orgasm? Did she bite him and scratch him like an excited cat? Was she now his girl? Would she continue to give it to him any time he wanted it? Would it always be under the old silk cotton tree or would he take her behind the church or behind the cinema? Hardly anyone did it under the silk cotton because it was alleged that the devil lived there, though it was always better to take girls to a place that they feared, a dangerous place where you could tell them you'd protect them and they would regard you as their hero.

The fellas envied him, but Leroi felt bad. He was assailed by guilt and shame and remorse. He had lied and tarnished the reputation of a good, morally upright girl, a church girl, a born-again Christian who had dedicated her life to God, to serving Jesus Christ, and paid little or no attention to boys; a girl who was probably an innocent virgin and would remain that way until she married someone with whom she would be 'equally yoked', as she liked to say. She liked to say to the older boys who hissed at her to get her attention or made sexually suggestive gestures in front of her that mentally she was far too old for them.

Leroi started to stay away from the fellas and to be very polite to Charlotte. She invited him to church and he accepted. He was happy when they passed by the junction on their way to church and saw them together. The doubters were dumbstruck, but the following morning those very doubters accosted him:

"We were hiding in the dark behind the silk cotton tree. You pass it straight, you and that church girl, talking about the sermon, you never stoop under it even to kiss."

"We knew you were mako-ing us," he told them.

He went to church with her on a regular basis and the pastor's sermon invariably included a tirade against the sin of fornication which, he claimed, would bring down God's wrath upon the island, for the island was unfortunate to be so full of fornicators. He made Leroi so terrified of the hell fire he was sure to be cast in if he ever fornicated that he stopped hissing at girls and fantasizing about 'doing thing' with them in his bed at night as he played with himself.

Then Leroi stopped going to church when

Dialectics called him a church boy and asked him if he didn't know that going to church was a most unfashionable thing, and that there was no God; that God and religions were constructs of the elite to deceive and control the people and keep them superstitious and backward, the better to exploit them; that religion was an opiate of the people; that the greatest fornicators were the pastor and other church elders and that the easiest girls to get were church girls.

"When I became a teen and begin taking an interest in girls," Dialectics said, "my godfather told me to join a church. It was the easiest place to meet girls. I join a church and encountered a god that was very partial, very unjust, very short-tempered; a god who it is said created all human beings but selected an ethnic group as his chosen people, a god that give away inhabited lands to his chosen people and encouraged his chosen people to carry out genocide against those native inhabitants and occupy their lands.

"I couldn't agree with this narrative and this god, especially as I was becoming politically conscious and learning that the Boers in South Africa were using this same argument that God made a covenant with them to dispossess the native Africans of their land. I argued frequently with the pastor and the elders and I get accused of blasphemy and being a heretic and not having faith and being an unbeliever. I wasted all my time arguing with these people and had no time left for the church girls. All those prayer meeting opportunities passed me by and I soon back-slided, a failed Christian with less faith than when I went in."

"So how you can say that church girls easy when you not speaking out of experience?" Leroi challenged.

"Since then I've found them to be easy. Some of them like the challenge of talking me out of my disillusionment and atheism; some are attracted by what they see as my badness, my sinfulness." Dialectics said.

Leroi did not find Charlotte easy to get, and his father was disappointed that he had stopped going to church with her.

"Stupid boy, that girl would'ha make you a good wife. One day she will make some other boy a good wife." John John said.

When Leroi told Dialectics that he had been going to church because of Charlotte and needed to keep up the pretense lest he lose her,

Dialectics said,

"Church girls don't make good wives; they can't wind. Unless she was a bad girl before she joined church. Clarissa used to be a church girl before she back-slided and started to meet me under the cocoa. I had to teach her how to wind."

"You're the devil." Leroi told him. "You don't believe in God."

"But the devil believe in God," Dialectics replied, "they complement each other as a duality. No devil no god, no good, no bad. I'm an atheist without apologies, comrade. I discovered the truth about organised religion. But you must discover their concept of god and their manipulation of that concept to suit their needs for control, power and wealth for yourself."

CHAPTER 16

January, 1980

SEVERAL of Leroi's peers were drafted into the newly formed People's Revolutionary Army. Joe John was among the first to join, against his mother's and father's wishes. But he told Leroi he was a big man now and could make his own decisions. He was a father now. Margaret had delivered their daughter even as Dialectics and the others were charging down that hill in True Blue to attack the barracks of the Defense Force and start the revolution. For that reason he had named her Dawn, a child born as the new dawn was breaking.

Leroi's father John John threw away all his precautions whenever he drank and refused to listen to Leroi's warnings and advice. Rum emboldened him and he criticized the revolution openly and loudly.

"They carry out a *coup d'état* and call it a revolution!"

"It's a revolution, Dad," Leroi argued. "It has

mass support."

"They are a bunch of rabid communists with more book sense than common sense," his father ranted. "America's rejection of their overture of friendship and refusal to give them aid did not drive them into the arms of Cuba and Russia. They decide to align themselves with Cuba and Russia long before they overthrow the government. Look at them now. They do away with the constitution and are ruling by decree. They used to criticize Gairy for traveling overseas on taxpayers' money, but today they doing the same thing and when they travel they bringing big contingent with them, so much bodyguard to impress their communist friends. They ban all newspapers but their own Free West Indian newspaper. They say we now have freedom of expression, so I talking, I'm expressing myself to prove it or disprove it. They promise to hold election in six months. Six months pass long ago and no election. This is the first betrayal of the revolution, boy. More is to follow."

Leroi, who by this time had been nicknamed Comrade, tried to stop him.

"Papa," he pleaded, "stop the drinking, and stop the criticizing. They will pick you up and shut you up, put you in detention, bring out the heavy roller and put you under heavy manners."

His father paid no attention to him.

"Look, son. They detain most of the people who founded the original JEWEL and many people who supported them during their struggle. That's gratitude for you! Beware, son!"

Comrade and his father almost came to blows when Comrade told him that he was going to join the army. He had not yet decided. He was only testing his father. He had not yet finished school.

They quarreled every day, especially in the evenings when John John began his drinking. Comrade began to resent him, for his friends began pointing out to him that his father was bitterly opposed to the revolution.

"Perhaps you are too," they suggested. This outraged him and he challenged them.

"How can you say that? I'm committed. I am a true revolutionary."

"Prove it," they demanded.

How could he prove to them that he was a true revolutionary? Could he prove it by attending militia training more regularly?

He reported for militia duties every day of the week and studied whenever he could. Lumpen made them abandon the old .303 rifles they had seized from the police and supplied them with the more modern M52 rifles. Later the AK47 would replace the M52 and Lumpen would describe it as the weapon of revolution and liberation struggles.

Dialectics said that the M52 was a gift from Cuba and that it was the rifle the Cuban patriots used to repel the Bay of Pigs invasion in 1961. The name Alfredo was scratched into the butt of Comrade's M52. When Dialectics showed the militia a Cuban documentary film about the Bay of Pigs invasion called Playa Giron, Comrade observed a young Cuban revolutionary he saw in a scene shot in a swamp. There was a burst of enemy fire and the young Cuban threw up his arms and fell backwards, the rifle slipping from his grasp. Comrade imagined this young Cuban to be Alfredo whose rifle he had inherited. He began to treat the rifle almost like a religious icon. This was the rifle of a martyr—a revolutionary martyr. When Dialectics spoke to the militia about fighting imperialism he imagined himself defending the revolution against the mighty superpower with his M52 and giving his life, if necessary, achieving martyrdom like Alfredo.

Then the M52 was replaced by the AK47, which came with its own romanticism. It was not handed down from any group of revolutionaries—Dialectics said that it came as a donation from Russia. Or was it Czechoslovakia or Bulgaria? Dialectics described it as a weapon of revolution, a weapon of liberation struggles like those in Angola and El Salvador.

With the arrival of the AK47s in the hands of young boys like his son, John John's disaffection with the revolution intensified.

"Don't bring that thing in the house," he warned Comrade the first time he carried his AK with him from the camp.

His criticism and condemnation of the revolution as a sham and the revolutionary leaders as delusional communist dreamers who would soon wake up to reality and turn on each other was so frequent and open that he was finally arrested and put in detention at Richmond Hill prison.

March, 1980

On the evening of March 13th, 1980, the first anniversary of the revolution, Dialectics called Comrade and Joe John and told them:

"I want you to accompany me to pick up a dangerous counter who may also be a CIA agent and a mercenary and put him under heavy manners."

Comrade and Joe John were eager to go. They hated counters, CIA agents and mercenaries. Comrade was surprised and alarmed when they drove into his grandmother's yard.

"What!" he cried. "You picking up me father?"

"Why not?" Dialectics said. "He is a counter."

"He is not!" Comrade said. "He just run his mouth when he drink his rum."

"You refuse to arrest your counter-revolutionary father?" Dialectics asked. "Are you a true revolutionary or not?"

"I'm a true revolutionary!" Comrade shouted.

"Prove it." Dialectics said and ground his teeth.

Just then John John came out into the verandah to see what vehicle had pulled into his yard.

"John John, you counter!" Dialectics greeted him. "You sleeping in Richmond Hill tonight!"

John John turned abruptly and made as if to go back inside. Comrade shouted at him.

"Don't resist, Baba. Don't bother to go for your bull pizzle, your cutlass or your gun. Just come with us, peacefully."

"What!" John John bellowed. "You ungrateful little wretch! You come to arrest your own father? I'll wring your neck!"

He charged out of the verandah like a mad bull. As he reached the jeep Dialectics drew a makarov pistol and pointed it at his head.

"Get inside the jeep, John John," he said, "your bad-john days as a brutal inspector of police are over now. It's detention for you. You're off to Richmond Hill."

As they were leaving, Grangran came out into the verandah.

"Where you taking me son?" she wailed. "OH LORD, Papa God, they taking me son to detention."

Comrade could not stop himself from standing up in the open jeep, his AK47 in his hand, crying out to his grandmother:

"Go back inside Grangran. Baba will be okay.

He will be released after a while. We will not harm him."

"You!" she screamed. "You have curse? How you could come and arrest your own father and take him to detention? What revolution would force a child to arrest his own father, Papa God? Put a hand, God, put a hand!"

She bent double, the better to stare at Comrade. She shouted, pointing and wagging a long, bony finger at him.

"Blood thicker than water! Son and children should honour their parents! What has your father done to you? Why have you sacrificed your father's freedom to prove your commitment to a bogus revolution?"

"The revolution is not bogus." Dialectics objected. "It is genuine, it is real, it is a big revolution in a small country. The first revolution of its kind in the English-speaking Caribbean!"

Grangran ignored Dialectics and directed her attention to her grandson, shouting:

"Your father has not done anything bad to you! Apart from the occasional slap or whipping, but those were for your own good! They were necessary for your discipline. In fact, your father loved you and protected you! Your father taught you to play cricket, he played football with you, he taught you how to lay trap for ground dove, how to make catapult, how to carve spinning top from guava wood, how to make windmill from the sides of cigarette boxes and kite from strips of bamboo! Your father taught you how to pitch marble and pick mango from the tall trees! Yet you arrest your father for the sake of some damn revolution!"

They drove out of the yard to the sound of her wailing.

"I know it is he that is making you do this, son." John John said to Comrade, referring to Dialectics. "I warned you about him. He is evil. This is his revenge for the things I did to him when he was a troublemaker and I was trying to maintain law and order."

"Shut up, John John!" Dialectics shouted.

They drove in silence all the way to St. George's and up the ridge to Richmond Hill prison. By the time they got there John John was weeping.

"For you," he told Comrade as he left the jeep. "For you, son. I'm weeping for you."

Comrade was moved by his father's tears and wanted to weep himself, but he could not weep in the presence of Dialectics and Joe John.

His father was taken inside the monstrous prison where over four hundred others were under heavy manners.

In the language of the revolution, 'under heavy manners' meant detention or any of the other forms of discipline or punishment the revolution adopted for its dissidents or suspected dissidents. The term was derived from a Jamaican political campaign song. Comrade loved to listen to the fast-paced rhythmic reggae song from which the phrase was taken. The song was a campaign song of the People's National Party of Jamaica which had sent many of their young self-described socialists and wannabe revolutionaries to Grenada to assist the local revolutionaries in their quest to 'build socialism' and undertake the transformation of the Grenadian society. Many of them ended up in broadcasting and exercised influence in programming and selection of music.

In the PNP campaign song the singer enunciates all the achievements of the PNP when they were given a chance to govern, in one verse, declaring in his Jamaican dialect 'socialist ah no fool!' Although there were programmes, policies and projects like free education, minimum wage, equal pay for women and the like that the singer declared were 'under manners' by the PNP ('*we avedem under manner, 'eavy, 'eavy manners!*'), the Grenadian masses reinterpreted 'manners' to mean discipline, particularly the punishment, for example by arrest and detention, of suspected counter-revolutionaries or 'counters', as they were invariably labeled.

When they got back to Camp Supplice the militia surrounded them. They regarded Comrade with awe.

"He arrested his own father and took him to detention," they said. "He is a true revolutionary in truth."

That night Comrade wept into his mattress on the floor of a bedroom in the haunted old great house. The following morning he avoided his comrades and took his plate of bakes and saltfish and his cup of cocoa tea outside to eat by himself under the long mango tree. He had no appetite. Joe John joined him and said:

"You're not eating, Comrade. Let me finish that breakfast for you. We can't let good food go to waste."

As Joe John ate, he said, "You must feel real miserable, Comrade. I would too if I were you.

I would never arrest any of my own parents to prove anything. My family comes before the revolution."

Tears fell freely from Comrade's red and swollen eyes as he hung his head in misery. He began to spend his days and nights in Camp Supplice until one day Joe John told him,

"Go home, Comrade. Your granny asking about you. She want you to come home."

That evening Comrade went home. His grandmother had cooked a pot of dumplings and peas and filled a bowl for him. It smelled and tasted delicious. It was the kind of soup he loved—dried peas, round dumplings and eddoes with saltbeef cooked in coconut milk. As he ate Grangran rubbed his shoulders and said to him,

"Come back home, me child. I know they forced you to do it. I have forgiven you. Your father will forgive you. Stop blaming yourself, stop hating yourself. Eat your food and go to bed. There is more food in the pot if you want some more."

"Thank you, Grangran," he said, but he continued to attend militia training regularly.

During the next two years, Comrade visited his father once. John John stood holding onto the grill of his cell, weeping and asking Comrade why, why had he done this vile thing? Comrade felt ashamed and guilty and the shame and guilt inspired defensiveness and a need to be spiteful. He shouted at his father the cruel words of a popular local calypso whose chorus had become a revolutionary slogan:

"Stand up dey and feel the weight o' the revo!"

His father crumbled as if from the weight of the revolution on his back.

"What have they done to you, son? What have they done to you, my child?" he sobbed.

CHAPTER **17**

IT was while they were training in the mountains above Gouyave where Julien Fedon, the revolutionary leader of the middle 1790s, had based the revolution he led under the watchwords 'Liberty or Death', that he met Gloria, the girl from Grand Roy.

Comrade was crawling on his belly through the undergrowth of an almost impenetrable elfin forest when he saw her crawling ahead of him. She was also crawling on her stomach and the most prominent part of her was her bottom. All of the rest of her was hidden by bush, but her bottom was exposed. When he caught up with her, he discovered that she was a beautiful golden-brown girl with dimpled cheeks, a friendly smile, avocado-shaped breasts and long legs. He said to her:

"Comrade, if this was a real war your bottom would'ha give you away. The enemy would'ha shot it off."

"Or he would'ha thrown down his gun and come crawling and slobbering to me, comrade," she replied and giggled, "who are you?"

He told her that his name was Leroi, but everyone called him Comrade because he loved referring to others as comrade all the time and because everybody saw him as a true revolutionary, a true comrade.

"And you?" he asked her. "Who are you?"

"Gloria of the Grand Roy militia," she told him. "I'm lost."

"I'm lost too," he said, "let's stay lost now that we found each other."

They lay beside each other and talked and talked. Gloria said,

"I don't know why we're in the mountains. The time for mountains is over now. It was over since the time of the marrons and Fedon. We should hold this maneuver on our coastlines. The enemy is going to come from the sea and the sky and if we retreat to the mountains they'll blast us out of them from the sky with their helicopter gunships and their bombers."

"The mountains were the fortresses of the marrons and the revolutionary forces of Julien Fedon, our folk hero."

"I don't know much about the marrons, except the fact that they were runaway slaves. I'm not too impressed by Fedon." Gloria said.

Comrade had never before heard anyone express any reservation about Fedon. He was surprised.

"Why? Fedon and them discovered the mission of their generation and set out to fulfill it. Theirs was a generation born in slavery, although Fedon and the other revolutionary leaders were born in freedom. They were mulattoes and were discriminated against by colour prejudice. Besides, they were Catholics and spoke a French patois and the colony was controlled by English Protestants who did not trust them. They understood the predicament of their people and discovered their mission to find a solution to it. They decided that this solution was to seize the island from the British and recreate a society where everyone would be free and equal. They failed to fulfill their mission, but they did not betray it."

"No." Gloria said. "They were defeated before they could. They fought no heroic battles. They just gave up the fight and melted away, every man for himself. Many were captured and hanged."

They talked about the Fedon revolution for some time and Comrade told her that he had composed a poem comparing the Fedon revolution to the March 13th one, which he hoped to one day perform at a Heroes Day rally or publish in the Free West Indian.

"Dare I call myself a poet?" he said.

"Why not?" she replied. "All manner of people calling themselves poets since the revo. Frantz Fanon, I think it is, said that revolutions release the creative genius in ordinary people and enable them to express themselves in ways they had never imagined they were capable of. That is why farmers, janitors, housewives and others have emerged as poets today, performing their poetry at village council meetings, rallies and other gatherings, getting them published in the Free West Indian and in anthologies of the revolution. Let me hear your poem."

Comrade was shy and reluctant at first, but after he had mustered enough courage he cleared his throat and recited it.

"They did not call one another comrades then
They called one another citoyen
It was the vocabulary of their generation
The language of their revolution

They had discovered their mission
They had discovered the solution
To their predicament
They took a solemn oath:
Liberty or death!"

"That's all?" she queried when he stopped reciting. "That's it?"

"That's it," he confirmed. "You like it?"

"Sort of. It's better than many I've heard. I guess you can call yourself a poet."

"You think so?"

"Yes, you're a poet, a revolutionary poet, as others are calling themselves."

"Thank you. I'll send in my poem to Don Rojas, the editor of Free West Indian, and I'll perform it at a rally."

"I'll be proud of you," she said.

The conversation gradually became personal.

"You have a boyfriend?" Comrade asked her.

"No," she replied. "Not anymore. I had a boyfriend. He was a teacher like me. I teach at a primary school. He left for Cuba on a scholarship to study medicine. The last time I heard from him he told me that he had met a Cuban girl and was thinking of marrying her and that he was sorry but I should forget about him and find someone else!"

"Well, comrade Gloria, you've found me."

"I don't know you."

"Don't worry. You'll get to know me."

Eventually they found their respective units and separated after exchanging addresses and agreeing to meet again.

"We'll fight side by side when the invasion comes." Comrade told her.

She agreed, but confessed her hope that an invasion would never come.

The invasion did not come and Comrade was deprived of an opportunity to bury imperialism in the sea. He had imagined himself standing on the beach, his feet planted firmly in the sand, his AK47 aimed at the sea, spitting bullets and saying 'Gracias! Grrrrrrrraaaaaaaaaaacias!' as the Cuban instructors claimed the AK said.

His world was now occupied with Gloria and in his imagination she was more beautiful, her legs were longer, her breasts were firmer, her hips were wider and her bottom was rounder and more prominent than ever. At nights he played out scenarios in his head, stripped her naked in his mind, buried his face in her pubic hair, or 'puel' as it was locally referred to, imagining it as being abundant, thick and black like the hair on her head.

He told his grandmother, "I met a girl from Grand Roi named Gloria and I like her a lot."

"She like you?" Grangran asked him.

"I don't know," he was forced to admit.

He wanted to know. He wished he had some way of knowing whether this beautiful, big-boned, full-blooded girl liked him the way he liked her.

One day, as he was drinking a cold Carib beer on the Lanse in Gouyave with a comrade from Grand Roi, he asked the comrade whether he knew Gloria.

"Which Gloria? Teacher?" the comrade replied.

"Yes, her." Comrade confirmed. "She is a member of the Grand Roi militia."

"I know her," the comrade said. "Just by looking at her a man could start to drool. But she is selfish. She keeps it to herself and doesn't give it to anyone, no matter how much you beg. She comes from a good family and they are staunch supporters of the revolution, true patriots. What happen, you like her?"

Comrade admitted that he did.

"I wish you luck," the comrade said. "Wha' you have going for you? You're not tall. You're not handsome. You're not rich. You don't have power or rank or education. Girls like that are not for you, Comrade. Take your mind off her. I see her and turn away and grind my teeth. I only take what I can get."

Comrade was convinced that he could get Gloria. He believed he had impressed her that time on the mountain. She had come across as a humble girl to him, though she was pretty and had such a voluptuous body. He didn't think she was vain, but sometimes he told himself that he did not deserve a girl like this, that such a girl was the reserve of more handsome men, men of wealth, men of power such as comrade Bishop and men of rank such as the senior officer in the army. Would a girl such as this give herself to a lowly militia man like him?

He told Joe John about her and Joe John advised him not to doubt for a moment that she would not give herself to him or that he deserved her. Afterwards he began to believe in himself a bit more and continued to ravish her in his dreams.

CHAPTER 18

March, 1982

COMRADE and Gloria met again on the following anniversary of the revolution when youths from all over the country gathered at Leapers Hill in Sauteurs to walk down the eastern and western sides of the island to Freedom Hill, the hill from which the attack on the barracks of the defense force was launched on the morning of March 13th, 1979.

She had linked up with him on the afternoon of the day before. They wandered through the town and went up to Marli to visit the People's Revolutionary Army camp at the Villa and the militia camp on an escarpment overlooking the town, also at Marli. The militia camp was a private residence that had been unoccupied at the time it was appropriated for use by the militia.

By evening time the town was teeming with youths from all over the country. They joined a crowd of youths dancing in the street to reggae music in front of Pato's Place. When they were tired of dancing they went up to Marli pasture and crawled under some blacksage bush and made love. The bushes were teeming with other couples doing the same thing, satisfying the same needs. Afterwards, they went back into the town, walked around for some time, and then went to the militia camp to sleep. All the mattresses were taken and there was no space left on the concrete floors of the bedrooms, the living room and the kitchen, but a comrade found them an old mattress and a blanket and they slept out in the verandah with other youths who were looking for somewhere to sleep.

They were up at 'foreday morning' and headed for Leapers Hill, the promontory over whose edge the indigenous inhabitants, the Kalinago, whom the Europeans called Caribs, had leapt in 1651 in a desperate act of collective suicide following a final heroic battle with French colonizers, preferring death to capture and enslavement. The romantic version of the account—the narrative that most fascinated Comrade—claimed that they shouted 'liberty or death!' as they leapt. That cry of liberty or death was later taken up by Fedon and his supporters, but in the end Fedon chose flight over death, unlike the Caribs. The Caribs had fought bravely against the colonists and had been driven to this promontory where they made their final stand.

Comrade thought of the heroism of the Caribs that morning as he huddled beside Gloria on the grass among a multitude of other youths. Below the promontory, the sea roared and waves crashed against the rocks violently. The sea here was always angry, always violent, and Comrade imagined it to be angry at history for being so cruel to people without power—people without the necessary military and other resources to defend themselves.

Albatross soared overhead and Comrade admired their wingspan and freedom. Gloria's head was resting on his chest, against his beating heart, and Dialectics was addressing the youths. He was saying,

"This is where it all started, comrades. This is where our history of struggle began. Right here on Leapers Hill. This is where our struggle against conquest, dispossession, slavery and colonialism began. This is the legacy the Caribs left us: *Liberty or Death*. Today we'll walk from Sauteurs to St. George's, retracing our steps.

We'll walk through plantations where once our ancestors were enslaved and relive their struggles to be free and reclaim their humanity. We'll walk through streets where once our people marched for higher wages, better working conditions, justice, equality, the right to an education and the freedom to express themselves."

Afterwards, a poet read a beautiful poem describing the revolution as a new dawn and praising it for the positive changes the poet said it had brought. Other poets performed their poetry, all in praise of the revolution. Some of the poets were middle-aged people who Dialectics described as 'workers and farmers' who had found their voice. Dialectics told the gathering that Frantz Fanon had written that revolution releases the creative energy in oppressed people and gives them the opportunity to express themselves in poetry and prose to the amazement of even themselves.

After the last of the poets had performed, a DJ played inspiring reggae music, mostly the music of Bob Marley and the Wailers. Bob Marley exhorted his listeners to '*open your eyes and look within*' and demanded '*are you satisfied with the life you livin?*'. Comrade opened up his inner eyes and took a peep. He saw three years of revolution and felt triumphant; he saw three years of his father's detention and felt mortified. When would this guilt leave him?

His spirit was dampened, but it lifted as he the rose up with the others to begin the march to the voice of Bob Marley singing *Exodus*, which he defined as the '*movement of Jah people*'.

He and Gloria took the western route. At Grand Roi she wanted to go home and rest, complaining that her legs were hurting her and that she was tired, but Comrade forbade her from dropping out of the march and would not agree to go home with her even after she promised to give him 'something good' if he came with her.

"The revo needs people who could endure to the end," he told her, "people who would not divert, who would not drop out, who would not lose focus. That's why we undertake this march."

She relented and soon they were labouring up Marigot Hill and marching through Concord, chanting revolutionary slogans with the others: "*A people united can never be defeated!*" and his favourite, "*Forward march, forward march, forward march against imperialism!*" They were chanting "*Stand firm, patriot, stand firm*" as they marched through St. George's. By the time they arrived at Freedom Hill in True Blue he was hoarse and his legs were weak. He and Gloria collapsed in a heap with other comrades on the grass.

Comrade lay on his back with Gloria lying half on top of him as Maurice Bishop and other leaders spoke, describing the foreday morning of March 13th, 1979 when they had congregated on that hill and launched their attack on the barracks of the defense force below to start the revolution, describing it as a glorious and heroic act. Bishop said:

"We are certainly proud of what we have achieved over these past three years, but we realize also that we are still on the threshold of the real changes that we want to see in our country. We have taken the first steps, and we have no room in our process for complacency or premature satisfaction."

In keeping with the custom of designating each year a special focus, he designated 1981 as the Year of Political and Academic Education.

At the end of the rally, Comrade felt confident and proud and very optimistic about the future and was satisfied that many of the other youths felt the same way. They boarded a truck and were driven home. Comrade stopped off in Grand Roi with Gloria, and in the gathering dusk they bathed in the clear cool water of the Grand Roi river.

Gloria's parents were not pleased that she had brought home her boyfriend to sleep with her, and her father asked him bluntly:

"I hear that you arrested your own father and put him under heavy manners for the last three years now. Is that true?"

Comrade was forced to admit that what the man had heard was true.

Her mother gasped: "Oh God, Lord, have mercy!"

Gloria's parents avoided him after that, but did not object to him spending the night. He was notorious, and he was dangerous. If he could do that to his own father, what wouldn't he do to them? He was a revolutionary and a member of the militia. He handled guns. They would not risk antagonizing him. That night he and Gloria went about their lovemaking quietly and the following morning he left early without saying goodbye to her parents and without having breakfast. He got a ride in a PRA truck full of friendly soldiers.

CHAPTER 19

COMRADE did not go with the soldiers to Camp Supplice. He went home to his grandmother's place. In the middle of the footpath that linked Clarissa's parents' yard with his grandmother's yard, Clarissa and Dialectics were quarrelling in stage whispers. She was gesticulating angrily and he was calmly defending himself against her accusations. Curious, Comrade sneaked up the footpath and hid behind a tamarind tree to listen.

"Liar!" Clarissa hissed. "You did not take the western route. You took the eastern route and you were all the time with that redskin girl from Grenville. Well, don't bother me. I not sharing any man. It's either me or her."

"It's you, Clarissa," Dialectics swore. "You and no one else. I have no intimate or romantic relationship with that girl. I can even introduce you to her. She is a comrade, a party activist, a revolutionary sister of the National Women's Organization, the NWO, that I'm always encouraging you to join."

Comrade understood Dialectics' problem. His woman was not active in politics and the activities of the revolution as he was. She did not like politics. Comrade compared her to Maurice Bishop's wife, who kept away from his politics while his mistress, Jackie Creft, was actively involved in politics and in the revolution. She was the Minister of Education and spearheaded the campaign to eradicate illiteracy through the Centre for Popular Education or CPE program. Ironically, Clarissa admired Jackie and was a volunteer teacher in the CPE programme, an involvement Dialectics applauded and felt encouraged by.

Comrade remembered how delighted Dialectics was a couple of days before the March 13th anniversary when Clarissa joined him and other volunteers in a community clean-up activity, debushing the roadside and cutting overhangings. Then she had joined them in the community beautification activity, helping them to paint the bridges, walls and even tree trunks with the national colours of red, green and yellow, painting red circles representing the new dawn, and writing slogans reflecting the aim, philosophy and projects of the revolution such as 'Each One Teach One', 'Women Equal in Education and Production', 'Who knows, Teach, Who don't, Learn', 'Education a Right Not a Privilege' and 'Every Worker a Learner, Every Learner a Worker'. But this was not enough. He could not discuss socialist ideology with her or party politics or the Cuban revolution or the struggle in Angola or what was happening with the House Repair Programme, the Free Milk Distribution Programme and the scholarships to the children of workers and farmers to study in Cuba, Russia, Bulgaria, Czechslovakia and East Germany to become doctors, dentists, economists and engineers.

Clarissa refused to join the militia, saying "I 'fraid the gun!" The saying was made popular by a calypsonian who won the crown with a calypso which described the fear his girlfriend had of his gun. '*When she see I charge it and I get behind it. She say no Survivor, no no no survivor!*' Survivor was the name of the calypsonian. The calypso posed the question: '*What you think she fraid?*' and answered with the line: '*She fraid the gun!*'

Some people expressed their disapproval of the proliferation of guns in the hands of young men by saying "I 'fraid the gun!" until it became a cliché. But Comrade knew that most calypsos were subtle in their composition and intent and were not to be interpreted literally. He had attended the calypso monarch competition and seen the calypsonian and his dancer acting out the *double-entendre* of the song, and had understood its double meaning. The gun was a literal gun, but could also represent the phallus, and the female dancer, dramatizing her fear of the literal gun which the calypsonian held suggestively at waist level, was also dramatizing her fear of the phallus—her dread of being ravaged by too big a *kukus*, as the male genitalia is referred to in Grenada.

Comrade wanted to come out of hiding and assure Clarissa that she had nothing to worry about, that Dialectics loved her and would not forsake her for another woman no matter how many he befriended and slept with, but Clarissa saw him hiding behind the tamarind tree and called out to him:

"Comrade, I see you, you mako. What you doing hiding there, eavesdropping? Why you so fass?"

Comrade came out from behind the tamarind tree and said to Clarissa:

"It's not me business and I know you go say I fass, but I can tell you I know that girl from Grenville you accusing Dialectics of friending with, and I know my comrade would not leave you for any other girl. So calm down and stop stressing the comrade."

"Mind your damn business and stop covering for David," she snapped. "All you men are the same and you're always covering for one another."

Chastened, Comrade walked off and left Clarissa and Dialectics to sort out their quarrel.

That very afternoon he saw them walking hand in hand with towels around their necks, headed for the beach to take a sea bath together. Dialectics winked at him and Comrade thought to himself that Dialectics would always have other women—he was handsome, educated and popular—but Clarissa would remain his main woman, his number one. He thought of Gloria and decided that she was all the woman he needed.

CHAPTER 20

March, 1983

COMRADE switched on the transistor radio on his bedside table and listened to Maurice Bishop's address to the nation in which he made the alarming declaration that 'an attack of imperialism' on the island was imminent. Bishop said:

> <<Tonight, on behalf of our party and government, I have the responsibility of informing our people that our revolution is in grave danger and that our country is faced with its gravest threat since our glorious March 13th revolution. From evidence in our possession, we are convinced that an armed attack against our country... can come any day now.>>

He changed into military fatigues and prepared to go out and do his patriotic duty of defending the country and its revolution.

The threat had always been external in everybody's mind in those days. No one imagined it could be internal, that it could come from within the party itself. He remembered how alarmed he was at the time after listening to Maurice Bishop explain that he had received intelligence that 'imperialism' was about to strike. It was always imperialism that was the threat.

He was more alarmed than he had ever been since the panic that was caused by the Amber and the Amberdines scare in 1981. He remembered the year because it was the year of the Heroes of the Homeland Maneuver during which he met Gloria, the girl from Grand Roy and lost his virginity.

The militia had gathered one afternoon at Supplice House. Dialectics spoke to them.

"United States Army Rangers are conducting a curious maneuver just off the coast of Vieques island, an island belonging to Puerto Rico. It is entitled 'Operation Ocean Venture '81'. According to the script there has been a revolution in Amber and soon enough there is a split among the leadership. The warring factions create a dangerous situation. The Army Rangers invade Amber to free American hostages and establish a new government that is friendly to the US."

Comrade was wondering about the relevance of this story when Dialectics asked the militia:

"Who do you think Amber and the Amberdines is referring to?"

Then Comrade experienced his epiphany and blurted out the answer that exploded in his head.

"Grenada and the Grenadines!"

"That's right, Comrade," Dialects said. "Grenada and the Grenadines. Imperialism is simulating the invasion of our country. This is a dress rehearsal. We are in great peril. Our leaders have gone on a political and diplomatic offensive to alert the world of the threat facing us and to call for international solidarity. They have informed the United Nations, the Non-Aligned Movement, the Organization of America States and other regional and international organizations about the grave situation and aggressive plans. The threat to our revolution is real and imminent."

"Let them come!" a defiant militia shouted. "Let them come!"

It was a call and the rest of the militia shouted

in response: "We will bury them in the sea!"

All that afternoon they chanted this slogan, marching on the spot out in the yard, their AK47s in their hands.

"Let them come! Let them come! We will bury them in the sea!"

Comrade loved his AK47. It was the weapon of revolution and liberation struggles all over the world, Dialectics had said.

"It is the weapon of choice of poor and oppressed people all over Africa, Latin America and Asia, so-called Third World peoples."

It was the rifle that would defend the revolution if or when the Amber and the Amberdines scenario played out for real.

Comrade was ready to die that time. Dialectics had commented on his zeal and dedication during the Heroes of the Homeland maneuver that was the People's Revolutionary Government and the People's Revolutionary Army's response to the Operation Ocean Venture '81 maneuver which they saw as a provocation and an attempt to intimidate them.

There were militia camps and occasional maneuvers all over the country so that civilians would receive military training to enable them to defend the country from mercenaries and from imperialism. The militia would bury them in the sea. The enemy was invariably described as external and people were programmed to expect them to drop from the sky or come in from the sea. So when in the week preceding October 19th, somewhere around October 12th, Dialectics called all the militia to a meeting and announced that he had solemn news for them, Comrade imagined that imperialism was about to invade the island and the militia were being prepared to fight and die. Instead, Dialectics told them:

"Comrade Bishop is no longer in power. He is no longer the leader of the revolution and the commander-in-chief of the armed forces. He is under house arrest."

The shocking news was greeted with shouts of:

"What? No longer in power? No longer commander-in-chief? Who is under house arrest? What you mean by that comrade?"

Comrade was sure that there would have been bloodshed had Dialectics not taken the precaution of disarming the militia. Most of them were ready to take up arms to go and release Bishop from his house arrest.

He argued with Dialectics, telling him:

"Comrade, you accused my father and others of being CIA agents and detained them in Richmond Hill prison without trial, but no CIA agent could ha' done a better job than you members of the Central Committee of isolating and destroying the revolution and offering up the country to imperialism. You are the real counter-revolutionaries, the real destabilizers! The real enemies! You are your own worst enemies. As that benighted Trinidadian writer said, you are dangerous only to yourselves!"

CHAPTER **21**

May, 1983

COMRADE and Gloria met again at a rally in Simon, an African Liberation Day rally at which the youths chanted: "*African blood is we blood!*" and listened to a speech given by Samora Machel of Mozambique.

They met up for the carnival Tuesday jump-up and he maintained a stiff erection as Gloria rolled her behind against his lap in time to a popular calypso about the infectious spirit of carnival on individuals, chanting along with the calypsonian: '*The comrade tell she, she have soca fever!*'

After the carnival was over, she followed him home. His grandmother welcomed her, but pulled him aside and hissed at him:

"You turn man now. You bringing woman in me house. Doh bring woman in me house. I wouldn't stand for it. You must have respect for me grey hairs. Don't take that girl in me house!"

He mumbled that it was this kind of attitude

of parents and grandparents that forced young people to go and 'do thing' under the cocoa and in canefields and bushes. He sneaked Gloria into his bedroom.

On this occasion he had a better look at her naked body. The sight of her pubic area excited him. It was so pretty. The fellas had often described the ones they saw as pretty. Some of them had described it as fat. This one was fat, fleshy, big. He got on top of her and she guided his manhood to where it belonged. Gloria moved rapidly under him in swirling curves. She was winding. The fellas were full of praise for girls who could wind. Suddenly, he felt himself climaxing. The pleasure was so exquisite, he couldn't hold back himself.

Gloria was disappointed.

"You come already?" she shrieked, scandalized, and clapped his head violently between her palms. "What kinda man are you?"

She sucked her teeth in that classical demonstration of disgust, the sound phonetically rendered as "cheups" or "struups", itself vocalizing disgust. It was this that hurt him. He felt dejected. He had failed. If Lumpen or the other fellas in the militia heard about this there would be no end to the teasing and taunting. They would say he was not a real man. Real men were men with the ability to satisfy women.

Although Lumpen was not handsome and tall, he had many women. The comrades said that before the revolution Lumpen couldn't get women, but that the revolution caused Lumpen to get women, for although Lumpen was ugly and stocky, the revolution had given him power and women were seduced by his perceived power. Lumpen was a captain in the army and had girls all over the island. He had them in the militia camps, and he met new ones at rallies, at walkathons, at blockos. What if Gloria told one of her girlfriends about his dismal performance and the girl happened to know Lumpen and share the scandal with him?

He felt an urge to make Gloria promise that she would tell no one about his failing. He was mustering the courage to approach her when, to his relief and gratitude, she told him in a voice full of compassion,

"Don't worry, Comrade. Sorry about my initial reaction. I didn't mean to make you feel bad. Next time you'll do it better. Practice brings perfect. Not all men are experienced in dealing with women, though most men pretend to be."

"Thank you, Gloria."

As he was sneaking her out of the house, his grandmother confronted them.

"You look like a decent girl, Gloria. You say you are a teacher. Beware my grandson Leroi. He arrested his own father and put him in detention."

Gloria nodded. She knew. Later, feeling guilty and ashamed, he tried to explain his actions to her.

"It... it... was in the early days of the revo," he stammered. "Dialectics made me do it to prove my loyalty."

"You shouldn't have listened to him," she said, "no one should be forced to arrest his own father to prove his loyalty to a cause."

Then she pestered him with questions. Was he eaten up by guilt? Was this why he seldom smiled and looked so sad and serious most of the time? Would he try and speak to Bishop to release his father?

He told her that he felt guilty at times, but was happy that his father was out of his way. Had his father been around, he may not be attending militia trainings so regularly. He may not be so active in the National Youth Organization. He would not have dared to bring her in the house.

October, 1983

Comrade had begun to spend most of his weekends in Grand Roi and he and Gloria bathed in the river together. He found out she was pregnant only during the crisis that began from around October 12th or 13th when people learned that Bishop was under house arrest and of a plot to kill him or depose him. Before then the comrades had teased him about his inability to get Gloria pregnant. They had called him a green coconut. He knew what they meant and it hurt him. A green coconut was not mature enough to yield any oil.

On the day that Gloria came to tell Comrade that she was pregnant, he met her outside the militia camp after Dialectics had disarmed the militia and informed them that Bishop was no longer prime minister and commander-in-chief of the armed forces.

"Comrade," she said, "why you looking so

sad and quiet? What troubling you? The militia come out of this meeting and everyone silent and glum. What happen?"

He told her what had transpired.

"The scriptwriter for the Ocean Venture '81 Amber and the Amberdine scenario must have been a prophet. Those comrades are today acting out that script. They are in the final act." Gloria swayed as if about to faint.

"I can't believe this," she gasped. "Maurice under house arrest? The revolution falling apart? My whole world is falling apart. I could feel the earth moving under my feet. Hold me, Comrade, before I fall."

That evening Comrade felt numbness, emptiness and despair upon realizing that the country had plunged into a political crisis that made the revolution he was committed to more vulnerable than it had been at any other time.

His spirits only rose when Gloria finally told him that she was two months pregnant. He was elated. He almost levitated. He had impregnated a woman. He was no green coconut. He was going to be a father. He was a man, a real man, even as he was a true revolutionary.

When he got home he found Grangran sitting

in her rocking chair in the verandah, gently rocking herself.

"I'm so happy to see you, son," she said. "Tell me what I'm hearing is not true. Tell me Bishop is not under house arrest and that the revolution is not split in two."

"Unfortunately, it is true, Grangran," he replied. "But don't worry. Everything is going to be alright. They are all big men, mature men, educated men. They will resolve their differences through reasoning, negotiation and compromise. They will reconcile and save the revolution."

"How could I not worry?" Grangran said. "These men are fighting over power and control and there is so much guns in their hands. What going to happen to us? I'm worried about what going to happen to us. I fear the worst. I wish your father was here. I'm worried about him too. What is going to happen to him?"

"Nothing is going to happen to him." Comrade said, and hurried inside to eat his dinner. She had cooked rice with split peas and had made a stew of fried jacks. Grangran came in while he was eating, her face a mask of worry.

"Grangran," he said, "Guess what: Gloria is

pregnant."

"For who?" she said.

"For me, of course," he said, surprised and indignant that she should ask that question.

"You could make child?" She said.

"Well, I damn well could!" he said. "I got her pregnant."

"You must be crazy. You making girl pregnant in times like these? These are uncertain times. This is no time to make woman pregnant."

He kept silent and she went away muttering to herself. He was happy he had distracted her from worrying about his father, but he felt deflated at the same time.

PART FOUR

CHAPTER 22

October 20th, 1983

DURING the curfew that General Austin had imposed following his announcement that Maurice Bishop and the other leaders had been killed in a crossfire, Comrade felt trapped in the Carifta Cottages. He wanted to go home. He wondered whether his grandmother had enough food in the house, whether she needed medicine from the pharmacy to control her diabetes, and whether Gloria was alright.

He kept the radio on all the time. The programming had been reduced to a desperate attempt to justify the tragedy that had occurred at the fort on that fateful day. PRA soldiers were interviewed and some of them broke down in tears as they narrated their alleged ill-treatment by Maurice Bishop on the fort that day. Comrade dismissed their confessions as mere propaganda. He thought there might be merit in the claim that the soldiers who had been sent in armoured cars to retake the fort were shot at. Yes, they were certainly shot at and the deaths of two of them, Mason and Cornwall, were being announced and mourned. They would be given a funeral. Nothing was said of the others who had died and Comrade wondered what had become of their bodies and whether their bodies would be handed over to their families for burial.

Just as he was wondering who was in charge, the radio announced the formation of a Revolutionary Military Council, and listed its members. He was not surprised to hear Dialectics' name on the list. He was wondering how this RMC was going to govern when Dialectics drove up in a military jeep, accompanied by a young brown-skinned woman in military clothes. Dialectics introduced her as Emma, a soldier in the PRA.

"She was on the fort that day," Dialectics said. "You must have heard her confession on the radio."

"Yes, I was in the operations room when Bishop and them came bursting in." Emma said. "He demanded the keys to the armoury and began handing out guns to civilians. I thought he was mad. He demanded that we soldiers change into civilian clothes and said he was starting a new army. I said I didn't want to be a part of this army."

"He wanted to wipe out the leadership of the party and army." Dialectics said.

"What is this RMC they just announced on the radio?" Comrade demanded. "There is no more People's Revolutionary Government?"

"We are in charge." Dialectics said. "We'll run things. The PRG is no more. It is dead."

"The revolution is dead." Comrade replied. "The people's revolution that began on March 13th 1979 is dead. It died on Fort Rupert yesterday."

"The revolution lives." Dialectics said.

"*Your* revolution. The revolution of the party, the revolution of the Central Committee, the revolution of the RMC. Not the revolution of the people—the popular revolution. Not the revo." Comrade argued.

"Whatever. Bring us some food, Comrade. You have food?" Dialectics said.

"I don't have food. I can't go out and buy groceries because of your curfew. You people have orders to shoot me on sight if I venture outside."

Dialectics ignored him.

"The Comrade who owns this place always have it stock up with food."

Dialectics went into the kitchen and was soon rustling up some rice and corned beef. As the rice cooked, Dialectics went into the drinks cabinet and helped himself to copious amounts of white rum. He gave some to Emma, who proved herself to be as accomplished a rum-drinker. She flopped down on a couch as Dialectics went into the kitchen to check on the rice boiling on the stove.

Comrade went up to Emma and handed her another glass of rum. He ambushed her with a direct question.

"You witnessed the execution of Maurice Bishop, comrade?"

She nodded.

"Yes, Comrade. It was horrible. They lined them up against the wall and shot them down. Some pleaded for their lives, some were silent like lambs, some fell fast, some fell slow. Afterwards, many of the soldiers who witnessed it were weeping and wailing and we were ordered not to leave the fort."

She began to cry and Comrade felt sorry for her. She must have been traumatized by the horror. Dialectics came out of the kitchen with three plates of steaming rice and corned beef. He saw Emma crying.

"What happen? Why you crying?" He demanded.

"The memory." Emma said. "It was so horrible."

"I told you to forget it!" Dialectics shouted at her. "Get over it! Drink some more rum. The rum will make you forget it. Come and eat. It's not good to drink rum on a hungry stomach."

They ate and as they did they listened to the radio. The death and funeral of "a comrade soldier Joe John" was announced.

Comrade was shocked.

"Oh God!" he cried, "Joe John dead? Poor Joe John. How did he die? Where did he die?"

"He died on the fort." Dialectics said. "He was riding on top of the first armoured car and was the first to be shot. He was shot across the chest. He died on the spot."

"I want to go to the funeral tomorrow." Comrade said. He felt so bereaved that he lost his appetite and could not eat anymore. He played with his food, squeezed too much ketchup on the rice and corned beef, and pushed the plate away from him.

After they had eaten Dialectics and Emma retired to the couch. Emma was all over him, kissing him, unbuttoning his shirt and rubbing his hairy chest.

"Rum always makes me horny," she confessed loudly.

They retired to the spare bedroom. Soon Dialectics returned in his underwear. There was a massive bulge at the front of it. He selected two cassettes from on top the music deck and returned to the room. Comrade remembered that there was a stereo in that room. Soon he heard the mellow baritone of Gregory Isaacs— the Jamaican crooner and composer of reggae love songs—coming out of the room, and the timely creaking of the bed springs as if keeping rhythm to the lovers rock.

Comrade mumbled to himself. "Love in a time of crisis. Love in a time of curfew. Love to the music of Gregory Isaacs, the love man himself."

All night long Gregory Isaacs crooned and the bedsprings creaked. As he fought to get some sleep, Comrade reflected on the ironies of life: rum caused some men to become impotent and was an aphrodisiac for others. There was a strong rum called Jack Iron that was reputed to give men a kick, in the coded language of men talk. Comrade had tried it once—before he made love to Gloria. He had confirmed the truth of the claim, for that night he summoned an energy and endurance he did not know he possessed and both surprised and delighted Gloria, who asked him afterwards: "Where did you get that kick?"

He did not tell her it was from Jack Iron rum. He did not want to give the rum any credit. He wanted it all for himself.

CHAPTER 23

October 21st, 1983

THE following day Comrade drove with Dialectics and Emma to Joe John's funeral. The roads were deserted. Occasionally they met PRA soldiers, but the soldiers waved them on when they saw it was Dialectics and Emma.

A soldier told Comrade in response to his query: "We have not shot anyone, though we see people using footpaths and tracks to go buy groceries or tend to their animals or visit one another."

At the church and at the cemetery, Joe John's mother was inconsolable.

"They kill me son," she sobbed, "me one child. They gun down me son like a dog."

Comrade went up to her and tried to console her.

"He died in action." Comrade told her. "He was on the first armoured car sent to retake the fort. He was killed on the spot. He didn't suffer."

She was indignant.

"He was not on no armoured car! He was not with those people. He was for Bishop! He loved Bishop! They killed him because he refused to join the firing squad and kill Bishop!"

Comrade realized that he was dealing with a family myth—a narrative that was more comforting to the family than the truth, one that depicted their son as a hero rather than an anti-hero, rather than one who had been on the side of those considered the bad guys. This alternative narrative would ensure that his memory was not tarnished. In this alternative narrative, her son had done the right thing, the conscientious thing. Comrade wondered who had told her the version she believed, this version of her son as a conscientious objector.

"There were people who saw everything that happened," she wept. "They told me what they saw. Joe refused to join the firing squad and kill Bishop and them, so the sadist psycho lieutenant who was leading the firing squad put a pistol to his head and shot him dead."

Was there any truth in that narrative? Comrade wondered and reasoned whether the RMC would be allowing Joe John the privilege of a funeral if he was killed for refusing to join a firing squad to kill Bishop.

A little girl he supposed was fours year old, Dawn, clung to the hem of Joe John's mother's skirt. She sucked her thumb and wept silently. Comrade felt sorry for her and wondered whether she understood the meaning of death or was aware that her father was dead and was being buried.

Joe John was being buried in the same cemetery he had often taken Margaret to when he was alive to 'do thing'. Margaret was sobbing inconsolably, holding her eighteen month old baby boy to her chest.

Comrade went up to her and told her to be strong. He noticed a small crowd gathered around the undertaker and gravitated towards it. The undertaker was saying:

"Yes, this is the only body they brought to me. The bodies of the other two soldiers were taken to the other undertaker. Otherwise, neither of us received any other bodies."

"So what happen to the other bodies? Are they still lying on the fort?" An angry man shouted. "My neighbour's daughter, who is a student, hasn't come back home since the 19th. She was in the demonstration. I heard she went up on the fort with Bishop. Her mother stands at the window looking out for her day and night. She don't sit, she don't sleep. She just waits by that window, hoping her child would come home. I went to Town and looked for the child in the hospital. She was not there. I checked with the morgue and I was told that no bodies were brought to the morgue."

A tall man spoke up.

"My brother who lives in Calivigny talk to me on the phone. He tell me that throughout the night of the 19th he smell smoke and wondered what could be burning whole night like that. He sniff and sniff and make out the smell of burning tyres, burning logs and burning flesh. There was a strong smell of burning hair. The next morning he saw this thin column of blue smoke rising over the tops of the trees in the area of Camp Calivigny. He could not imagine what could be burning there and who could be burning it. He knew that the camp was empty. All the soldiers had been taken away in trucks and brought to Fort Frederick. He wondered why they had been removed. Was it to facilitate this burning? He became suspicious and suddenly thought he knew what was being burned. They were burning—"

"Don't say it!" A woman pleaded, interrupting the man. "Don't even imagine it. Such a thing can't happen in this country. We respect the dead too much for that."

"Ah..." the tall man said, "then let this be a time for self-discovery. We never imagined that we capable of gunning down civilians or lining up our leaders against a wall and shooting them without mercy. We are what they call a close-knit society where everybody know everybody else and we take it for granted that all o'we is one family, but look what we up and do to one another: open fire on civilians, execute popular leaders by firing squad, impose shoot-on-sight curfew on the population, burn instead of bury dead bodies. On the nineteenth, family ties meant nothing, camaraderie lost its meaning and solidarity. I heard that Jackie Creft appealed to the members of the firing squad by referring to them as comrades and asking them to reconsider. I heard that one of them retorted *'no comrade in these effing times or no effing comrade in these times'*. Not even her informing them that she was pregnant could soften their hearts or win her some sympathy. There goes our saying that all o' we is one family!"

"Hush!" The woman hissed. "One of them is coming!"

The small crowd dispersed quickly as Dialectics approached. He was looking for Comrade.

"I'm ready to leave," he told Comrade. "I'll take you back to Carifta Cottages and drop off Emma in Woburn or Woodlands or wherever she want me to drop her off."

Comrade was relieved that she wasn't going to spend another night at the cottage. He'd had enough of creaking bed springs all night in sync to the music of Gregory Isaacs and her loud and wanton cries of "Woioioi! Gi me! Gi me! Gi me!"

He was walking out of the cemetery when he heard his name being shouted.

"Leroi! Leroi!"

It was Grangran. She came hobbling towards him.

"Leroi, me child, I was worried about you. I thought you was dead. I stayed in the church after the service to pray and me macmere Bertha come and tell me she see you in the cemetery."

Comrade was happy to see her too.

"Grangran, you all right?" he asked her. "I

kept thinking about you, alone in the house, unable to come outside because of the curfew, wondering whether you have enough food, whether you need medicine."

"I'm alright, son," she said. "Papa God is with me. This young man here, David, Bertha son, come by and told me don't be scared and offer to go get me grocery and anything else I need. He is a good boy, David."

Dialectics smiled shyly. Comrade turned to him and said, "Thank you, Dialectics."

"It's nothing," Dialectics said.

CHAPTER 24

ON the way down to St. George's, Emma annoyed Comrade by saying,

"Bishop is not the saint you and most other people think he was. In fact he was very selfish. The masses loved him and risked their lives to free him from house arrest. And what did he do? How did he show his gratitude? He led them to a military installation to surround himself with them and use them as a shield, as fodder, whilst he went about his business, making phone calls, stripping soldiers of their uniform, breaking into the armoury. I confronted him. I asked him what he was doing here, why he had brought the people here. I told him he was responsible for this mess."

"History will absolve him." Comrade said.

"Oh," she said, "he too? I thought it was only Fidel Castro! I hope you do not write this history."

"Why not?" He replied. "Your story must not be the only version. I must tell mine as well."

Comrade had heard a story that no order

had been given, but that a grieving and enraged soldier with the rank of lieutenant, angry at the killing of his comrades who had been sent to retake the fort from Bishop and his followers, had executed them. So why had this soldier not been arrested and court-martialed? Why had General Austin tried to cover-up the dastardly deed by claiming the comrades had died in a crossfire? Why the attempt at a cover-up? He tended to believe a third narrative that claimed that orders to execute had been given by a young colonel after consultation with other officers and members of the Central Committee and wondered whether Dialectics was among them.

He reflected that General Austin had declared a twenty-four hour shoot-on-sight curfew and the people were too terrified, disillusioned and demoralized to go out and fight if the country was attacked. The militia all over the island had been disarmed. Who would re-arm them? He felt frustrated and trapped in history. He understood that this day in history marked the end of the revolutionary era he had been a part of and he felt caught up in the moment as he had felt on March 13th 1979, but this time he felt like an insect caught up in the web of history, with the dread of the spider consuming him.

As they approached Grand Roi he begged Dialectics to allow him to see Gloria briefly.

"Just to say hello," Dialectics said. "No hugging and kissing and you-know-what."

Gloria was in her verandah and Comrade ran up the steps to her. They met in an embrace and she kissed him hungrily.

"I'm so happy to see you, Comrade," she said. "You're alive. My child's father is alive."

He rubbed her belly.

"How is it?"

"It's coming along. I get sick every morning and I can feel it growing in me."

He lifted her skirt and kissed her naked belly.

"Let's go inside," she suggested. "It's been a long time. I miss you."

"There's no time," he said, "and, as you know, I'm not a woop-wap man. I love to take my time."

"Too bad!" she said, then added, "I can't get over this curfew. I can't believe they turned the guns on the masses and executed Bishop and them. They were all comrades. What went wrong?"

Comrade had no answer for her and Dialectics began to blow his horn impatiently, so he and

Gloria gave each other one last hurried kiss and parted.

"I give you an inch you take a yard." Dialectics protested as they drove out of Grand Roi.

As they entered St. George's they were challenged by soldiers guarding the Green Bridge around by Queen's Park and at the entrance to River Road. The soldiers recognized Dialectics and allowed them to pass. Other soldiers were positioning a big gun that looked like a cannon on the Esplanade, pointing it to the sea. As they drove up to the roundabout on top of Lucas Street near the Governor General's residence, Comrade saw other soldiers placing big guns into position.

"All you preparing for war, comrade?" he said to Dialectics.

"All you?" Dialectics replied. "You're excluding yourself? Yes, we expect imperialism to attack and we must all be prepared to defend the country and the revolution."

"How do you expect us to do so when you disarmed the militia and have us all under twenty-four hour shoot-on-sight curfew?" Comrade said.

Dialectics ignored him. They dropped off

Emma in Springs at her boyfriend.

"Does he also do it to the music of Gregory Isaacs?" Comrade asked Dialectics. "You're horning the comrade, Dialectics!"

"He is a major in the army," Dialectics said. "He behaves as if he is God's gift to women. Don't feel sorry for him."

Comrade didn't feel sorry for him. He probably deserved Emma and she him.

"But what about Clarissa?' Comrade said.

"What about her?" Dialectics replied. "She is not speaking to me. She is not giving me. She doesn't even want me to visit my child. She want me all to herself, want to control me. I can't let a woman control me like that."

Comrade invited Dialectics inside to have a drink of rum with him when they got back to Carifta Cottages. Comrade really wanted answers to some questions that were troubling him.

"Dialectics," he said as they sat drinking in the living room, "where were you on the 19th when all those events were taking place?"

"I was with other comrades of the Central Committee and the army in the verandah of comrade Coard's house."

Comrade remembered that comrade Coard shared a yard with comrade Bishop. The houses were located in the same compound.

"We were there when the demonstrators arrived. We were expecting them. They pushed against the big strong iron gate and rattled it. There were soldiers on guard and an armoured car was in the yard, but we had ordered the soldiers not to shoot at the people. The soldiers shot into the branches of the trees. The demonstrators retreated, but when they realized the soldiers were firing into the branches and not at them they rushed at the gate again and hurled themselves against it. The gate gave way. They swept the soldiers out of their way and rushed like a breaking wave into Bishop's house. They came out carrying him and Jacqueline Creft on their shoulders, chanting '*We free we leader!*' The soldiers allowed them to carry Bishop and Jackie away. They didn't not trouble us. We learned that they were taking Bishop to the market square to address a crowd of his supporters waiting there. We went up to Fort Frederick.

"We were surprised and filled with anxiety to hear that Bishop had taken his supporters to Fort Rupert instead of to the market square. From Fort Frederick we could see people crawling all over the fort like crazy ants. We were alarmed. This was our military headquarters and we learned that Bishop had taken over the operations room and demanded the keys to the armoury. We wondered about his motives and intentions. We feared he was seeking a military solution to our problems and intended to wipe out the leadership of the party and army.

"We decided to dispatch two armoured cars to retake Fort Rupert. Joe John was on the leading armoured car. I bade him farewell and wished him all the best. They were not expecting any violence. They rode on top of the armoured car in the open. We despaired when we heard that the armoured cars were fired on as they approached the entrance to the fort. We heard the sound of battle and saw civilians leaping off the ramparts of the fort to their deaths and realized that things had gone out of control.

"I almost collapsed when I heard that Meyers, Mason, Dorset and Joe John were killed. Later, Lumpen, who had left on the second armoured car, returned and told me that Bishop and other comrade leaders were dead. He was traumatized and was acting and talking like he had lost his mind. *'Am I insane, comrade?'* he kept asking me as he wept. *'who was firing at us? Why were they firing at us? I found myself in the lower courtyard when I came to my senses. I was holding my AK in my hands and it was spitting bullets as if on its own accord. In a fog of smoke from a burning vehicle I saw people falling, leaping and twisting and folding as they fell. My nose was filled with smoke and the smell of gunpowder and blood and sweat and fear. I felt disgusted with myself and horrified at what I was seeing and doing. I flung the gun away from me, wanting to distance myself from it, wanting to distance myself from me. That's when I fled, comrade. That's when I fled from myself. That's how I know I'm mad'.*

"You're not mad, comrade,' I told him, *'You're just traumatized and need some rest.'* I led him away to get some rest. He kept reminding me that the madhouse was not far away and I should commit him there.

"I did not see him again until the night of the 22nd when he came seeking me out. He was quite insane. He told me that if anyone sends me to Camp Calivigny I should not go there because of what I may witness. *'What?'* I asked him. '*The horror,*' he told me. '*What horror?*' I asked him. '*The horror of the pit,*' he told me. I wondered: The pit? '*The pit of fire,*' he said. '*The pit of burning bodies. The pit of hell.*'

"All this was incomprehensible to me and I concluded that he was quite mad, which he was. Later that night a soldier told me that Lumpen had thrown himself down over the side of the fort in an attempt to commit suicide. We took him to the hospital. Some of his ribs, one leg and his right hand were broken. The emergency room was crowded and a doctor told me that they only mended broken bodies not broken minds and suggested we take him to the madhouse. But he was only speaking in jest. He attended to Lumpen and assured me that he would live if he healed.

"I feel as broken as Lumpen, Comrade. I suppose the whole country feel as broken, in body as well as in spirit. Pass the rum."

They drank and Comrade imagined that plenty of rum was being drunk all over the country, that plenty of ganja was being smoked and plenty of prayers being said.

As Dialectics was leaving to return to Fort Frederick, he told Comrade,

"Put away the rum, Comrade. We must stay sober. The revolution is in great peril."

It is not. Comrade thought. *It doesn't even exist. It died on the 19th.*

"When do you think imperialism will attack, comrade?" he asked Dialectics.

"Any time from now," Dialectics said. "Could be tonight, could be tomorrow morning."

PART FIVE

CHAPTER 25

October 26th, 1983

COMRADE looked out of the window and saw helicopter gunships landing on Grand Anse beach. Then he saw a black bomber roaring towards the cottages, perhaps heading for Point Salines and Calliste where most of the fighting was taking place. Suddenly he heard a loud explosion and the cottage shook. He took a wild glimpse outside and saw swirling dust and smoke, where only a minute before a cottage had stood. He threw himself on the floor as another explosion tore another cottage apart.

"Oh God!!" he cried. "They bombing up Carifta Cottages! Why? Why they doing that? This is not a military installation! Have mercy on me, oh God!"

As he prayed, a helicopter gunship thundered overhead and he heard the staccato sound of a machine gun.

"They strafing us now, oh God!" he cried.

As bombs fell and bullets rained from above,

Comrade lay flat on the floor on his belly, his hands covering his ears to keep out the sound of death and terror. He felt trapped and as helpless as a cockroach fallen on its back. He heard shrieks and wails. He realized that he was afraid of dying, he who had imagined himself fearless during militia training and willed the enemies of the revolution to come was afraid of dying now that bombs were exploding all around him and the sky was raining bullets.

As a bomb exploded a nearby cottage and bullets tore into a nearby roof, he grabbed his head, pressed his stomach to the floor and screamed, "Mama! Mama!" He was referring to his Grangran. He needed her protection now. She had always offered him protection.

He wondered now how many poor defenseless PRA soldiers were lying facedown under the picker trees of Point Salines, Frequente and Calliste, digging a grave for the living with their bare hands and calling on their mothers as bombs exploded around them and bullets rained from the sky.

Why are they attacking Carifta Cottages? He wondered. *This is not a military installation. This is a residential area. Did they have intelligence that comrades live here and wish to kill them in their cottages? Were they attacking other residential areas?*

He was seized by terror and felt the same awe he had experienced years before the revolution when he was still in primary school.

A friend of his, Clifford, had connections with the United States. He was born there and spent holidays there, in New York. His father was in the U.S. army and Clifford spoke of one day joining the modern army, as he called it, when he grew up. His father had completed two tours in Vietnam and Clifford was very proud of him. Clifford had this glossy army magazine. It contained glossy photos of modern weaponry that caused Comrade to gasp, and pictures of military planes, helicopters and battleships that filled him with awe.

He concluded that any country that was able to invent such weaponry and design, manufacture and possess such planes and ships must be mighty, and he was filled with awe and began to think of the United States as a mighty super power, but not as a foe.

It was not until the revolution, years later, that he began to think of it as a formidable foe because Dialectics said it was a foe. But even as he chanted '*Let them come, let them come, we will bury them in the sea*' during militia training, he remembered the might that those glossy photographs of modern weaponry, military planes, helicopters and battle ships represented. But he was not afraid then. During those times he believed that revolutionary fervor and patriotism alone could defeat such might. He drew confidence from his M52 rifle— the M52 which replaced the ancient .303 rifles confiscated from the police on the morning of the revolution, and which was replaced by the AK47.

He wished he had his AK47 now. Then he would not be cowering on his belly on the floor, holding his head. He would be leaning out of a window firing at the helicopter gunships. A drizzle of bullets shattered the glass louvers of a window facing the sea and he crawled under the dining table like a congoree, thinking he would surely die today.

Would his father cry for him? He couldn't imagine his father crying for him. His father was a hard and unforgiving man. His grandmother would cry for him. She would band her belly and bawl. She was forgiving and loved him unconditionally.

Would Gloria cry for him? She would grieve, he told himself. She loved him and she was carrying his child. If he died he would not get to see the child, to cradle it in his arms and rock it gently, and the child would not know him— would grow up without knowing him—and Gloria would be taken by another man.

The thought filled him with jealousy. *No other man deserves Gloria*, he thought. He wondered where she was now. She must be home listening to the radio announcing that the country was under attack and calling on the population to come out and defend the country.

The radio was making precisely such an announcement now. Suddenly the broadcast was interrupted and an ominous silence ensued. *What could be responsible for this abrupt silence, this rude interruption?* He wondered. It was not because of a power cut or low battery. He suspected that the radio station had been attacked and bombed and was filled with horror at first, then anger. Radio Free Grenada was his favourite station. It had started by proclaiming a revolution and had now ended denouncing an invasion, blasted into silence.

After about an hour he crawled from under the table and stood up. The air was polluted with smoke and dust. He peeked out of the window. There was destruction and desolation outside. Several of the cottages had been totally destroyed. He felt thirsty and went to the refrigerator to get a drink of iced water.

Comrade stayed in the cottage for two more days until he was satisfied that it was safe to move out. When the firing and bombing ceased, he dashed out of the door, leaving all his possessions behind. He saw marines setting up a base on Grand Anse beach and helicopters hovering above. He saw broken bodies lying out in the yard, and a naked brown woman, insane with fear, grief and rage, pacing about, tearing out her hair and wailing.

He ran all the way to town. Helicopter gunships were buzzing about Richmond Hill and Fort Frederick like dragonflies. A building was on fire. A wounded helicopter plummeted to earth, towards Tanteen. In town civilians were looting stores.

He leaned against the Farm and Garden building to catch his breath and watched a thin man carrying a huge refrigerator on his shoulders and a sack of flour on his head. The man staggered under the weight. *They will loot every store in town today,* he reflected, *except bookstores. The looters always leave the bookstores alone.*

He saw PRA soldiers exchanging their uniforms for looted civilian clothes and concluded that they were done with fighting or had not seen any action at all in the first place. *What cowards! What unpatriotism!* How he wished he had joined the army. He would have been fighting now, engaging the enemy down at Point Salines or Calliste or Frequente or True Blue.

What would he have been doing fighting? Defending the revolution. *What revolution?* The revolution he loved and had committed all his energy and time to had ended a few days earlier on October 19th, the day Maurice Bishop and the other leaders with him were executed.

As far as Comrade was concerned, what remained of the revolution was anti-people, hostile and unpopular. Perhaps that was why the

PRA soldiers had not stayed to defend it. Perhaps they were uncertain about what they were really defending; what they were risking their lives for. Still, he felt like fighting and felt contempt for the PRA soldiers who were exchanging their military fatigues for looted civilian clothes.

There was still one valid reason left to fight for, to sacrifice one's life for—the sovereignty and dignity of the country. He would fight for the sovereignty and dignity of the country. It would be the patriotic thing to do.

The soldiers were all unarmed. Where had they left their guns? What had they done with them? Had they left them in their barracks? Had they discarded them on the battlefield? Their hands were now filled with loot and they were in their looted civilian clothes, heading for home.

Comrade headed for home too, but without loot. The sky was a beautiful blue, but it belonged to the bombers and helicopter gunships.

CHAPTER 26

IN a pasture on the outskirts of the village, marines were slithering on ropes and rope ladders onto the ground from a hovering black helicopter. Other marines lounged around on the ground. A crowd of curious girls and young women stood around, watching the soldiers, advertising their availability. Comrade wondered what it was about men in uniforms that attracted women to them, or was it the gun they were attracted to or the power that the uniform and gun represented? Why had they come out in their Sunday best to pose before the soldiers? Some of them were already flirting with the soldiers and wore soldier caps and helmets.

A marine approached him—a dark brown young man of his age, with frizzy black hair. He chewed gum. He pointed his M16 rifle at Comrade and commanded,

"Halt!"

Comrade halted.

"Who are you?"

"My name is Leroi Pascal."

"Where are you going?"

"Home."

"Where you come from?"

"None of your business."

The marine did not take offense. Comrade noticed that his name tag read 'Nuñez'.

"Where you from?" Comrade asked him.

"Puerto Rico," the marine said. "This is the eighty-second Airborne Division from Fort Braggs. Come with me."

Nuñez led him to a man sitting in the pasture, surrounded by marines. The man looked defiant and considered the marines with hatred and contempt.

"Como se llama?" A marine shouted at the man and when the man refused to answer, he demanded: "Answer me, Cuban pig!"

"He is not a Cuban," Comrade said.

"Well, he has the beard, he has the look. Some Cubans are dark like you and him, even black like my friend here from Alabama. Who is he?"

"His name is Dialectics. He is Grenadian. We are from the same village."

"He was armed when we stopped him," an African-American marine explained. "He was in civilian clothes, but he was carrying a Makarov.

Is he a soldier?"

"No, he is only a revolutionary, a party activist. Let him go!" Comrade said.

"Don't tell us what to do!"

After some consultation among themselves, the marines decided to let Comrade and Dialectics go home, even offering them some little cans of combat food as a gift.

"As you know, brother," Nuñez said to Comrade as he left, "We've come here to save lives. We are liberators."

"I don't know that." Comrade said, but he imagined that many people, perhaps even his grandmother, would consider themselves liberated and rescued from an uncertain fate.

As Comrade and Dialectics walked home together, Comrade broke the silence.

"They came with overwhelming force, comrade," he said, "as we've always known they would come. We are no match for them. We have no bombers, no military helicopters, no battleships. Their soldiers outnumber our soldiers and are better equipped. What are we to do? Our soldiers are demoralized and our people are disillusioned."

"We'll have to surrender," Dialectics said in a

whimper.

Comrade had never heard him sound so defeated, so sad.

"Before the heroic stand? Are you not going to fight to the death? Are you not going to be heroic to the end?"

"Expect heroism from yourself." Dialectics said. "Not from someone else."

Comrade considered what Dialectics had said and could not come up with a suitable answer to it, so he said,

"Your generation has betrayed its mission, comrade!"

Dialectics looked at him and began to weep. He wept silently as they proceeded along the lonely road.

"Don't cry, comrade. There is nothing to cry about. It happens all the time. Time changes our lives and turns it to history and puts distance between those of us who lived it and those who will remember it or research it or study it or even record it and interpret it."

"Since when you become so philosophical, Comrade?" Dialectics demanded.

"Since I lay on the cold concrete floor of a room in one of the cottages expecting a bomb to fall on it any second. Recalling the details of my life and trying to interpret their meaning before I die." Comrade replied.

"And what good that knowledge would'ha done to you if you had died, Comrade?"

"Perhaps it would'ha done me no good. But enlightenment even in the last moment of life before you die is important. It brings closure."

CHAPTER **27**

"Dada!"

Dialectics' little daughter was playing in his parents' yard as he and Comrade walked in. The child ran into his arms. He swept her off her feet and kissed her cheeks.

"Where is your mother?" he asked the child.

Clarissa came hurrying from around a corner of the house.

"You asking for me?" She said. "You miss me?"

"I miss you." Dialectics said.

"I glad to see you alive." Clarissa said. "Me and your parents was in mourning because we hear a rumour that you had been killed in a battle around Sugar Mill."

"Rumours!" Dialectics said, shaking his head. "Grenadians love to spread rumours. There was a battle around Sugar Mill but I did not participate in it. I did not participate in any battle."

"Glad to hear that," Clarissa said, "but your eyes red and swollen. You were crying?"

"Maybe I was." Dialectics said.

"I would not be surprised if you were." Clarissa

said. "There is so much to cry about and not enough tears, even if the entire nation should start crying at once."

Loud voices rang out from the rumshop. Rum drinkers were arguing. Comrade strained his ears to listen.

"They calling it a rescue mission. They calling it an intervention. I say it's an invasion!"

"It's a rescue mission and an intervention. They have saved us from ourselves."

"Oh shut up and go and put a padlock on your wife and your daughter crutch!"

"Put a padlock and a chastity belt on yours too. I was in Trinidad in the 50s when the Yankees had a base in Chaguaramas. They turn all them Trinidad women, mother as well as daughter, into the Jean and Dinah that Sparrow sang about in a calypso in which he describe them as posing around the corner. Right now our Jean and Dinahs are in the pasture posing for the marines."

"Well they used to pose for the PRA. They love men in uniform and with guns."

"They love men with cars too and with money in their pockets and sweet talk on their tongue."

"And a big kukus in their pants."

The last remark drew laughter, bawdy laughter, and someone said,

"Well I have a big donkey one and women 'fraid it. I does call it the cribo 'cause it black and thick like a cribo when it ready to crawl. You know cribo like warm, damp hole."

"Oh, pass the rum and shut you damn mouth. Women say you can't do anything. You have a big one but you don't know how to use it. Mine is small but I know how to play it around. Women keep coming back for more. They tell one another about me."

"You dirty boaster! You liar! No more rum for you. I buy this round. Don't drink me rum!"

"Oh Lord, Papa God! The country is being occupied by a foreign army and all you people can do is talk stupidness and drink rum. Shame on you! If Bishop was alive—"

"Ah, if Bishop was alive we'd not ha' been sitting in this rumshop drinking rum and ole talking. We'd either be dead by now on a battle field or in the mountains or the bush fighting guerilla war."

"Good thing Bishop not alive. A lot of Grenadians would'ha dead in the fighting."

"If Bishop was alive there may not have been

any intervention."

"Invasion!"

"Whatever!"

"How will you all remember the revolution?" One rum drinker asked the others.

"It brought out the best in us and the worst in us," an old man said. "People were unselfish. They gave of their time and energy freely and worked together for the common good, in the community self-help programme, in the community beautification programme, in volunteering as teachers in the Centre for Popular Education's eradication of illiteracy campaign, and in many other ways. And yet there were others who abused their authority to arrest and detain others, to harass and torment others and finally to line up our leaders against a wall and execute them by firing squad. Something unprecedented in our history. Something we never imagined our people were capable of. So yes, the revolution brought out the best in us and the worst in us."

No one disputed him.

As Comrade was bidding farewell to Dialectics and Clarissa and their little daughter, he saw his grandmother hobbling out of Miss Bertha's shop, carrying a bag. She saw him and cried:

"Leroi, me son!"

"Grangran!" he shouted. He ran to her and embraced her.

"Me grandchild!" she wept. "Me one grandchild! I was grieving for you because I heard that you dead. Thank god you're alive. Thank you, Papa God! Thank you, God, for bringing those yankee soldiers to rescue us. They are in me yard right now, son and I come to the shop to get them cold drinks. We must always be kind to our visitors and offer them something to eat or drink."

Comrade took the bag from her and they walked home together.

There were marines in his grandmother's yard. Marines were sitting on the verandah, marines were picking mangoes off the coute mango tree in the yard, and marines were surrounding a man. The man looked familiar, but Comrade did not recognize him. His face was gaunt and lined with age, his body looked thin and emaciated, and he was bearded like a billy goat. But the man turned, saw Comrade and recognized him instantly. He got up from the ground and rushed toward Comrade, shouting:

"Leroi! My son! Leroi, you're alive!"

"Baba!" Comrade cried as he flew into his father's arms. "Baba you free!"

"I'm free," his father said. "These marines here rescued me and freed the other detainees. And you're alive. I hear there was a big battle at Bousejour and many militia, mostly from Grand Roi and those places died in it. I hear you was in that battle and was killed or had died in Carifta Cottages or in Frequente or in Celliste or at Point Salines."

"I'm alive, Baba."

"Yes, you're alive my son, and I thank God for keeping you alive!"

"Is that the son who arrested you and had you put in detention all these years?" A marine queried.

"Yes," John John replied. "He is that son, my own flesh and blood. I am not proud of what he did and I'm sure he is not proud of it as well, but there are things I've done that I'm not proud of myself."

The people of Grenada have healed from the trauma of the implosion of the Grenada revolution. They have forgiven those they perceive as being responsible for the failure of the revolution and have moved on. Today, Grenada is a stable democracy and there has been smooth transition of power since 1984.

The benefits of the revolution are manifest in the high level of literacy the country enjoys today, in the number of local people who were trained as dentists, doctors, engineers, etc. during the revolution, and in the Maurice Bishop International Airport, which was a project of the revolution. Those who were charged and tried for killing Maurice Bishop and members of his cabinet on October 19, 1983 have been freed and reintegrated into the society.

There is an abundance of material available for readers who want to learn more, on the internet and in print, including testimonies and interviews of those who were directly involved. There is also an emerging canon of literary works inspired by the revolution and its demise. This one is only one of them.

David Franklyn, who also writes as David Omowale, is a Grenadian writer and poet. His anthology of poems *Tongue of Another Drum* (1994) was published in Jamaica. His non-fiction works include *Bridging the Two Grenadas* (1999), *Morne des Sauteurs: Encounter Between Two Worlds in Grenada, 1650 – 1654* (1992) and *Ancient Egyptian Wisdom for Potential African Leaders* (2003).

His first novel, *A season of Waiting* (2002), was long listed for the International IMPACT Dublin Literary Award. His second novel, *Children of the Sea* (2009) was published by Heinemann in the Caribbean Writers Series.

David Franklyn works for the United Nations and lives in Nairobi, Kenya, with his wife Martha and three children.

CPSIA information can be obtained at www.ICGtesting.com
Printed in the USA
LVOW06s2148250614

391665LV00001B/23/P